A DEATH IN VEGAS

CHRISTOPHER MEEKS

White Whisker Books
Los Angeles

For my readers and for the students I teach.

ISBN: 978-0-9836329-9-3
Library of Congress Control Number: 2014902801
Copyright © 2014 by Christopher Meeks

First Edition

Editor: Lynn Hightower
Associate editor: Carol Fuchs
Book design by Deborah Daly

PUBLISHED BY WHITE WHISKER BOOKS, LOS ANGELES, 2014

Applause for *Blood Drama*

"*Blood Drama* is highly entertaining and extremely enjoyable. It is a combination black comedy and crime novel." —**Lori Lutes,**
She Treads Softly blog

"Meeks may have daringly stepped into new territory, but he continues to remain in the rarefied atmosphere of fine contemporary authors."
—**Grady Harp,**
Literary Aficionado

"*Blood Drama* is very much a thriller, but it is a thriller with a romantic twist. Protagonist Ian Nash is not an easily defeated man. He is a winner in spite of himself, and we love him for that."—**Sam Sattler,** Book Chase

"I loved this book from page one. The story spun here was so delicately woven, it kept my rapt attention from start to finish."
—**Krystal Milton,**
*Defining Women's Evolution
in Discovery* blog

"*Blood Drama* is a marvelous action thriller that culminates in a gut-wrenching life-or-death climax."   —**Jim Chambers,**
Top 50 Reviewer, Amazon

"My keyword for Christopher Meeks is 'authenticity.' As an award-winning dramatist, he knows theatre from the inside-out, and his frequent quotes from David Mamet add a savory sub-strata of wit and wisdom to *Blood Drama*. Mainly, though, he unfailingly entertains!"
—**Gerald Locklin**
author of *The Vampires Saved
Civilization)*

"I really enjoyed this novel, and I honestly hope it winds up being the first book in a series featuring the two main characters."
—**Kristina Davis,** Goodreads

"Well-written and fast-paced, *Blood Drama* is a lot of fun."
—**Laura Thomas,**
FUOnlyKnew blog

"This is a thriller, a page-turner with a noir edge and elements of a romance woven in—and it is much more.   —**Joy Renee,** *Joystory* blog

"It has been said that it takes ten days to form habits. Only ten days! If we take pains to persevere for ten days, we will be well on our way to good and Godly habits."
—Lorraine Curry, homeschooling expert

"I don't have any bad habits. They might be bad habits for other people, but they're all right for me."
—Eubie Blake, composer and musician

CHAPTER 1

Under the hotel's sheets, hands on his chest the way the dearly departed lay, Patton Burch blinked into the void of the ceiling, staring past it to the night before. He smiled. After drinking too much the previous evening, he had still remained the gentleman—except in his dreams where he'd made love to Chatterley. Should he feel guilty? Probably.

He turned. The other side of the bed was now empty. He'd slept so well, best in months, that he hadn't heard her get up. The sound of the hotel's shower, gentle as a rain, swept into the room. Chatterley's clothes, which she'd slept in, lay as if hastily discarded on the floor. What if she was feeling better, amorous, even? He pictured her showering, comfortable in her body that men craned their necks for. The truth of the situation was that he was now sober, and she was young, vulnerable. The last thing she needed was an older guy taking advantage of her.

Patton lifted the sheets and saw his boxers were on. He didn't remember getting out of his clothes. He did remember how Chatterley had trouble breathing last night, and between the drinking and another shot from her inhaler—a bronchial dilator, she called it—she'd been feeling sick again. She'd thought that strange. "I sometimes get shaky after using it," she said. "It's like having too much coffee, but I've never felt nauseous like this." She wanted to close her eyes for a few minutes, so he'd offered his bed. "Thank you," she said. "I just need to relax and catch my breath."

That led to her falling deeply asleep on his bed. He let her be. He'd mixed himself another gin gimlet and watched a Star Trek rerun. Captain Picard was on a planet where he had a wife and family. He wasn't a starship captain anymore but worked as an iron weaver, and no one believed him that there was a space vessel called the Enterprise. He came to love and accept his new family and let go of his past life.

After that, Patton had been too tired and dizzy to stay up. He remembered checking on Chatterley in the bedroom, hearing her breathe steadily and easily. He'd thought he'd just lie on the bed in his clothes, but here he was under the covers. He wasn't used to drinking, but it was Vegas. Ah, the fantasy of it all: a woman like her in bed with him. But he had to let her go. He loved his wife—and he wasn't like his father.

He could still smell grapefruit on the sheets. When he was a kid and even skinnier, for breakfast his mother would painstakingly cut each section of grapefruit halves for her family. Each pulpy chunk, cut from its heart wall, could easily be scooped up carousel fashion, one by one, and the sour sweet juice could be slurped. He loved that smell. In his dreams, there was something so pure and innocent about Chatterley's small tight frame, naked and fruity, that their lovemaking seemed as fun as the first time he'd floated down a freshly snowed hill on a sled. In dreams, we get what we need.

Chatterley was showering now. Maybe he should step out and let her have some privacy. He sat bolt upright. Was his wife due in this morning? No. Maybe tomorrow. He held his chest, feeling the pounding of his heart. Calm down. Nothing had happened. As he thought about the situation more, it wasn't as if he told Tess everything he did anyway. He'd snuck out to a few afternoon movies over the years and never mentioned them, and she certainly never asked. People could never be completely transparent to their mates.

The shower was completely steady sounding. He sat up, frowning. When someone's in a shower, movement makes the sound vary. Wasn't Chatterley in it? Patton turned his head toward the bathroom door. It was open. That's why the sound was so loud. "Chatterley?" he said. No answer.

He swung his legs over the side and stood. They hadn't closed the thick curtains against the daylight, so the western light, filtered by rare cloud cover, gave the beachscapes on the walls color. Outside, the gentle clay-colored hills far to the west looked flat. Considering that nothing green grew naturally in this area, Las Vegas was an unnatural place for a Lawn and Garden show, but this show was the biggest.

On her side of the bed on the floor, Chatterley's purse was upside down with everything in it spread out, including a few coins, her friend Faith's keychain, and a few panty shields. It was as if she had been desperate for something. Perhaps she'd merely kicked it accidentally. Then he saw her inhaler was in two parts: a small aerosol can and the blue plastic part that the can fit in. He picked up the can. It was empty. She must've been looking for another. Why hadn't she awakened him to help?

He strode into the steamy bathroom. "Chatterley?"

The room had both a large whirlpool bathtub for two and a separate shower with a glass door. She wasn't in either, though the shower was still on, pouring out steamy water. How could she leave it on? He turned it off, and the silence made her absence that much more profound. Did she step into the living room for a moment? Perhaps she'd put on a hotel robe and zipped to the pool. But without a suit? She could be topless in her panties, and the guests would love it. It was Vegas. She had beautiful breasts.

He could hear the air conditioner, a wide unit wedged into the wall near floor level in the living room, with its fan on high. As he moved toward the room, he was freezing with only his shorts on.

He stepped into the living room and saw her, near the Stratocaster, crouched naked on her knees before the long wide air conditioner. Her hands outstretched like a swimmer scooping the cool air. It looked erotic. "There you are," he finally said, wondering about her intentions. He really couldn't act on them. "Are you really that hot? Are you okay?"

She didn't move. Was she asleep? Her head, between her arms, rested on the thick carpet. "Chatterley?" he said and kneeled down to her level. He touched her to wake her, and his first thought was she shouldn't have been in front of the air conditioner so long because her skin felt downright cold. He shook her. "Chatterley." She splayed onto her side. Her eyes were open. She didn't appear to breathe. She stared skyward as if frozen in surprise.

CHAPTER 2 (DAY 1)

The day before had been his birthday, his forty-second. With more than eight hours on the convention floor and only Cheetos and a ham sandwich taken from the Scotts Miracle-Gro booth for fuel, the first day's work was done. Along with his sales crew, Patton had shown beneficial bugs to industry buyers at Las Vegas's Lawn and Garden World, part of the National Hardware Show. His company, BenBugs, "The Organic Choice," had a large and cherished corner display area with no tables. It stood at the intersection of two green-carpeted aisles, which, like two intersecting rivers, had brought people steadily to his shore. Two more days to go, but the first day of selling had ended with a bang. After a phone call, it was time to get himself a celebratory dinner at Envy, a nearby elegant steakhouse. He could feel it: his life was about to change.

As he stepped outdoors from the Convention Center, the heat slammed into him. Even in May after five p.m., Vegas was hot. He didn't want to walk far, after all, and Envy was in the Renaissance Hotel just across the lot. He was originally going to go to the Stratosphere because he loved the view as well as the food, but fuck it; a juicy expensive steak nearby was in order. As he walked across the huge parking lot toward it, his cell phone vibrated in his pocket. He pulled the phone out and saw it was his wife.

"Tess," he said, feeling particularly happy.

"Great news," she said, equally bright.

"You got Birnam to fund our expansion?"

"Venture capitalists always think they can own you."

"A problem?" he said.

"What the fuck, Patton? Why do you assume I create problems? I said good news."

"So tell me." He shook his head. Sometimes she did create problems, but she'd never admit it.

"I hammered out all the final details today."

"Do we still have controlling interest?"

"Who was the one who insisted on that?" she said.

"So you did it?"

"Yeah. Hey, hey."

"When do we get the money?"

"He has to go over the terms with his accountant and attorney. Papers should be drawn up in days. After that, very quickly. He'll wire it. Ten days tops. It's done."

"Wow. You're amazing," he said. Good. It'd been his idea to get a partner to grow nationally. They had deals throughout the West, but now with this and what just happened at the Convention Center, they might even go public someday.

"There's always the unexpected, but, yeah, we're done," she said confidently. "Consider it your birthday present, my handsome man."

"No Porsche?"

"I have something better, my love." He could picture her sitting with her evening glass of wine in their living room. She was probably in one of her elegant pantsuits, having kicked off her spiky heels. Thirty-eight, four years younger than he, she still looked great, often working out at the gym, and she shared his love of snow- and water-skiing. Her clothes gave her command in her sales calls. She sold with the tenacity of a boxer with the cheer of a game show host. He knew she thought of herself as running the company, but the fact was, BenBugs was his idea, which she originally thought was silly. "Chemicals are what made our food supply great, and you should stay in chemicals," she had said then. "The tried and true." She was pushing modems in those days and was the top salesperson in her company. She had always been tops in sales. She also could be wonderfully sexual.

"How's the convention going?" she now asked. "How's the ladybug girl turning out?"

"She's fine."

"Just fine?"

He knew she wanted him to say her "sex sells" idea worked. What the hell. Compliments were free. "All right, she's fabulous. She drew in the guy from Target, Wayne Jones-Bradbury."

"That fat fuck?"

"I took him through our line, gave him our brochures, and he agreed to meet us next week in Los Angeles to consider our bugs for all their stores with nurseries nationwide."

"Shit. Next week is fabulous. I can't believe both of these things happened at once. And good things come in threes."

"We both did well." He wanted some acknowledgement.

"I could kiss you all over," she said.

"Really? Is that my present?" Perhaps these fortunes would translate at last to the bedroom. He'd stopped initiating of late because she kept saying she wasn't in the mood or was tired. Change of life, she said. A guy can take only so many no's, even from his wife. Perhaps these business wins would be a kick to her hormones. That would be a third good thing. "I haven't eaten all day. I'm going for a steak," he said.

"Try Envy. It's in the Renaissance right by the convention center."

"I'm already headed there."

"Good minds think alike," she said.

"Yes," he said. "Might you make it to the convention tomorrow?"

"Let me finish up with our lawyer tomorrow for Birnam. Maybe I can make the last day. If I can't, the staff will help you, right?"

"See you when I see you," he said.

"You okay?" she asked.

"Just tired. Your news is good, though."

"Maybe you should go play your guitar," she said. "I love listening to you play."

"Thanks," he said. "Sleep well."

When he stepped into Envy, the restaurant cheered him up more: red patterned chairs, cherry wood paneling, and big basket lights that made him blink.

There at the curved bar in a lounge chair sat a ladybug—or, rather, Chatterley, the woman they'd hired to be a ladybug at his booth all day. He smiled. Her costume was designed like a sleeveless French maid's outfit with black platform shoes. Her long red stockings that ended mid-thigh and the tight red bodice each featured black dots. A black tutu spread like a lace umbrella from her waist, and her shoulder-length dark hair curled like a movie star's. Chatterley had pulled in many people all day. The booth's traffic was the best ever. Even the geeks at the electric-death rat zapper booth across the aisle had stared at her continuously. Sex sold.

On the barstool, Chatterley sat on one leg and had taken off her antennae and wings, talking intensely with another woman her age, mid-twenties. The woman wore black pants and a white halter-top and appeared concerned. Should he approach them? No. They were probably into some boyfriend problem or fretting over which dance clubs to hit that night, and who was he but Chatterley's latest employer? He knew a hello would be awkward. He needed to stay focused, think more about Jones-Bradbury.

He left the restaurant. He'd go back to his original idea, the Stratosphere. In front of the hotel, a yellow cab pulled up, and Patton waved to it. The driver nodded. Just as Patton approached the rear door, a hairy, bearded man in a sleeveless black t-shirt and black leather pants raced over and opened the door, shoving his tattooed girlfriend in. "Hey," Patton shouted. "That's my cab."

"I don't see you in it," said the guy, glaring and sizing him up. "Get another."

"No. The driver nodded at me, and it's my cab. There are rules." Patton pointed to the woman in the back. "Get out. This is my cab." The woman with far too much mascara looked raccoon-eyed at her boyfriend. The man, either a bass player for a metal band or a bad conceptual artist, spun around and punched Patton hard in the shoulder. Surprised, Patton turned to a doorman in a red uniform and shouted, "Are you seeing this?"

The doorman shouted back, "Get the next cab," and hurried inside.

The bearded man was moving into the car, and Patton knew that he probably shouldn't do anything, but this wasn't right. He grabbed the man's arm and said, "This is my cab!"

"Fuck you," the man said before smashing Patton in the stomach with a hard left fist, then a right into the side of Patton's head. "Go back to the slots with your grandpa-goes-to-the-mall shoes."

The man shoved himself into the cab and shouted, "The Stratosphere." The taxi took off.

Now on the ground, Patton held his head and stomach, forcing back nausea. His ears were ringing, and he was sure he was going to vomit right on his black tennis shoes. Grandpa goes to the mall?

He felt hands gently lift him under each armpit. "Are you okay?" came a sweet female voice. "My God, we saw the whole thing from inside."

Patton set his eyes on Chatterley, who continued lifting on one side, her friend on the other. Chatterley looked like a spotted angel in her ladybug costume.

"Yeah, what was that guy's problem?" said her friend.

The doorman was now there, breathing hard. "I just heard," said the man. "Are you okay?"

"Of course I'm not okay," Patton said, coughing. "You chickened out."

"I had to go inside."

"Who's your boss?"

"Would you like a free drink at the bar?" the man said. "I know the bartender."

"Mr. Burch, let's go to the bathroom first. There's a little blood by your ear," said Chatterley, now guiding him forward. Patton shoed the doorman away.

A flash went off. Chatterley's friend handed him his own cell phone, which had a camera. "I found it on the ground," she said. "Thought you might want a picture in case you sue."

"This is my friend Faith. Faith, Mr. Burch."

"Call me Patton," he said. He stood on his own power now, breathing deeply, pain now morphing into embarrassment. What the hell made him think to grapple with someone as big as a Bonneville?

"Faith and I worked together at a small local casino."

"I still work there," Faith said. "Patton?" said Faith. "As in the general?"

Patton rubbed his stomach, which felt as bruised as old bananas. "Yes. Patton is my mom's favorite general from World War Two." He extended his hand to finally shake. "You know your generals."

"Thanks to my dad," said Faith. She caught sight of someone over his shoulder, and smiled. "My friend's here. Gotta go." Faith waved to the someone.

Patton turned. Walking up the sidewalk, a young man in baggy tan shorts and a gray sports shirt smiled as if he had pulled all cherries on a slot machine. His glow could run the city lights for a week.

Faith squealed, then reached into her small purse and pulled out a single key on a keychain with a single silver heart on it. She put it in Chatterley's hand. "Take it," said Faith. "I won't be home anyway."

"Thanks," said Chatterley. "

"See ya," Faith said and ran off with a smile.

"Nothing like young love," said Chatterley, looking after her friend wistfully.

"What's with the key?" he said.

"I'm staying at her place tonight. Mine has problems."

"Problems?"

"Here," she said. "Let's get you cleaned up in a bathroom."

"That's okay. I'll just go to my hotel," said Patton.

"Don't be silly. You're bleeding. Get inside."

He was impressed.

They walked back into the restaurant, and Chatterley directed him into the men's room, which she entered, too, not seeming to care. No one was in there. She pulled out a paper towel from the dispenser and wet it. "Lean on the sink," she said. "I'll get it."

She dabbed gingerly near his temple, focused like a nurse. "This would be a great city," she said, "if it wasn't for all the people."

"I was stupid."

"No you weren't. Here, stay still." She kept dabbing. "You look good now."

"Maybe I need to be punched more often."

She smiled, and he noticed what a truly great face she had—oval with a nose that a sculptor could love, a gentle curve at its top. "You told me earlier you're going to college."

"College of Southern Nevada, a community college."

"So...what's your major?"

She shook her head. "After a day like today, you don't need to hear about that."

He let it go yet also felt he had to do the right thing. "May I buy you dinner for your help?"

"I know you're a busy man."

"I suppose you're meeting someone anyway."

"I was going to eat alone."

"Then have dinner with me. You're my savior."

She looked at him earnestly, then nodded.

They left the bathroom and moved up to Envy's entrance. As they waited for a hostess, Chatterley smoothed out her costume. "So how do you catch ladybugs?" she asked.

He shook his head. "I don't catch any. I order them from specialists who know how to catch them in the woods. They swarm."

"I seem to have lost my swarm."

"So I get you to myself. I'm lucky."

"Thank you."

After they were seated and looked over the menus, she ordered organic salmon and three jumbo prawns. He selected the prime porterhouse with grilled onions and mushroom sauce. They shared a bottle of wine, a pinot noir from Chateau St. Jean that Chatterley had suggested was undervalued. Patton slathered butter on the small cut-up baguette. "Sometimes bread is just the perfect thing," he said. "And it's sourdough."

Chatterley took a piece. "The best sourdough is Boudin's. Did you know they've been using the same starter for over a hundred and fifty years?"

"I don't know much about bread."

"Starter's what makes sourdough special. Most bread is made with flour, water, and commercial yeast. Sourdough has what's called a starter, which is water and flour that's allowed to sit around and feed off the natural yeast and bacteria in the air."

"Very organic," said Patton.

"Yeah." Chatterley coughed at that moment, held up her hand, and, from her purse, pulled out a blue inhaler. She yanked off the white cap, inserted the base into her mouth, and pushed down on the aluminum cylinder that sent out a burst of her medicine. She inhaled.

Smiling, looking better, she continued: "The bacteria in San Francisco, lactobacillus sanfrancisco, is what gives the perfect sour taste and makes San Francisco bread the best."

"You need an inhaler in Las Vegas? I thought the desert was good for asthma."

"Maybe something at the show irritated me—though it started yesterday."

"I'm sorry if the show did."

"Not important," she said. "Bread's important. The staff of life. A hundred years ago, bread was made at home. The smell of fresh bread is just..." She inhaled deeply as if pulling in the warm scent. "I love it."

"You know a lot about bread."

"I'm in a culinary program, didn't I tell you?"

"No."

"In my college. I want to be a chef."

"You don't want to be America's Top Model?"

"No. This may sound silly, but I didn't do anything to earn how I look. Food and wine is my calling—like yours is bugs. Isn't it great to be doing what you love?"

He nodded, though he wondered if bugs were his true calling. He'd always followed his curiosity, first into chemistry, then into this, but he always felt he had a lot more things he wanted to know. "I was reading a book called The Outliers," said Patton. "The author, Malcolm Gladwell, claims that people really good at what they do, like Bill Gates and the Beatles, have spent at least ten thousand hours at it. That'd be about four years if you worked at it eight hours a day, six days a week. I certainly did that in chemistry and bugs."

"I'm getting there," she said.

"Well, when you're my age, you don't necessarily have ten thousand hours to put into a new field."

"You're plenty young," she said. "Don't be silly."

When their entrees arrived, they each envied what the other ordered and traded bites. She asked him how he got into beneficial bugs, and he told her how he helped invent chemical compounds and pesticides used in agriculture before he created this new business, which was doing something better for the planet. "I really wanted to do something good. I want the earth to be a better place in fifty years. Wouldn't it be great if we weren't polluting our soil, air, and water so much?"

"Did you hear that scientists are trying to grow meat?" Chatterley said. "I heard on the news that meat might be hooked up to special nutrient tubes—cells divide, and, bam, you have a chicken breast."

"Would you eat such a thing?" he asked.

"I don't know. If you grill it perfectly and use the right sauce, it could be great, right?"

They both laughed, and Patton ordered another bottle of wine that she chose. Talking with her was quite easy.

— ❧ —

The idea was that she'd come to his suite for a nightcap. Her car was still in the parking garage of the convention center, so he suggested she drive it over to his place. She thought it was a good idea, but asked if he could drive because she was feeling a little sick, perhaps from the asthma medication. He'd suggested he drive her home, but she said she was going to stay the night at Faith's later.

"Isn't she going to be with her boyfriend?" he said, remembering how Faith galloped off after the guy.

"That's the point. But I'd enjoy a nightcap with you."

He didn't push it or ask why she was staying away from her place. He recalled how Chatterley and Faith had been so serious when he first saw them at the bar. If it was about that, he didn't need to make her feel so grave again. He felt good with her and didn't want the night to end.

The sounds of her platform shoes echoed rhythmically on the concrete in the parking structure. A hundred young men would love to vie for her attention, yet it was he who was there.

She tripped, and he caught her by her waist to steady her. "There, there," he said.

"I'm sorry. These shoes."

"No need to apologize."

"My protector."

In the few remaining feet to her blue four-door Kia, shiny and well-tended, he thought how he'd expected a far different evening, alone. For one, he had planned to call his sales people and prepare for tomorrow. Plus there was the refinancing still happening—and other things. Yet he didn't care. He felt alive. He shouldn't make everything about work. Sometimes you just had to appreciate the beauty of life. He held her hand and loved that she squeezed back. She looked happy, perhaps expecting him to make a move, but before anything happened, he opened her car door. There was a moment there where she paused before getting in, where she gazed at him as if grateful and willing to reward. He held back, just to be sure.

As he entered the driver's side, he noticed her costume's wings and antennae on the back seat next to a hardback book with a plain blue cover. "Reading something good?"

"What?" When she looked at the book, she said, "Oh, that." Frowning, she reached back and shoved the book under the driver's seat. "My insurance. I don't want to even think about it right now."

Patton wondered what kind of insurance came in a book. She seemed complex, this young woman. Soon her frown turned to a smile, and she squeezed his shoulder. He drove the few blocks to the Edison Suites Hotel, and he found a parking spot right in the front. As they ascended to his tenth-floor lodgings, the sexual tension rose like the elevator. As he smelled her fruity perfume, he just didn't want this feeling to end. She smiled as if feeling the same.

"Mind if I take your picture?" he asked, pulling out his cell phone.

"Really?" and she posed with a lively expression as if she were a Sports Illustrated swimsuit model.

When they reached his room, he swiped his card key and opened the door to the living room area. It was an elegant space with thick white carpet, paintings of beachscapes on the cream walls, a wide window that overlooked the monorail line below, a golf course, and the lighted strip a few blocks away. The air conditioner unit near the floor blew cool air below the bottom of the curtain.

"You play guitar?" said Chatterley. She pointed to his white Stratocaster in the corner near an easy chair and couch.

"A little," he said. "I find it's a good tension reliever."

"So you have a lot of stress?"

He nodded. "At times."

She stood and moved close to him. "Do you have a lot of stress now?"

He looked at her, smiling. "I probably need to play the whole Led Zeppelin songbook at this very moment."

Her face brightened, and she moved closer. A head shorter than he, she placed her hands on his shoulders.

"You smell like grapefruit," he said.

"I use a grapefruit sea salt scrub—Trader Joe's."

"Sea salt scrub." He pulled her closer and brought in her scent. As easily as a hawk glides, he leaned his face downward and found her lips. They kissed and embraced with the passion of songbirds in a willow tree.

CHAPTER 3 (DAY 2)

When a hard knock came to the door, Patton stood and swayed for a second, dizzy. The room's table lamps, all on, seemed too bright. The hotel security guy had arrived ten minutes earlier, a skinny man whose name on the six-pointed Security Guard star said "Henderson." In his late twenties with a crew cut, he strode past Patton to the door.

Henderson opened the door, adjusting his posture straighter as if to impress. Two young, uniformed policemen stood on the other side, one a tall, gangly Hispanic man, more like a scarecrow, with a nametag that said Jimenez, and the other a burly coffee-skinned man whose tag said "Kelly." His stare suggested he'd slap the nose off Patton's face if Patton said the wrong thing. Patton stood in place, wondering what to do with his hands, which felt as out of place as fish heads. "Metropolitan Police" read the policemen's arm patches. Both officers eyed Patton as if they had their man.

"Officer Jimenez," said Henderson. "I don't know your partner."

"This is Officer Kelly—new from New York." Henderson shook Jimenez's hand as well as the hand of the other cop, Kelly.

"This is Patton Burch," said Henderson. "He woke up, and his girlfriend was dead. She's over there." Henderson pointed.

"She's not my girlfriend," said Patton. "She was working for me."

"Call girl, you mean?" Jimenez pulled out a notepad and pen.

"No, I mean I have a beneficial bugs company, and she was working for me at the convention as a model."

Jimenez made a few notes. "So your employee was spending the night?"

Patton paused at the odd sound of the question, then nodded. "She'd felt sick. When she fell asleep, I let her stay. Nothing intimate happened."

Officer Kelly went over to Chatterley, who was covered by a shiny blue bedspread, which Patton had yanked off the bed. Patton had not wanted her spread-eagled for the world. Kelly pulled the blanket back, and his eyes flared in surprise. "She wasn't lacking in the looks department. Nothing intimate, you say?"

"That's not nice," said Patton. These men seemed like frat boys in uniform. He could be their father.

Kelly extracted what looked like a tissue box from his pocket, tugged out a single latex glove, and inserted his hand.

"Can you describe how she died?" asked Jimenez, looking over at his partner, who had his gloved hand on Chatterley's neck and shook his head. No pulse.

"I don't know how she died. This is how I found her when I awoke."

"Naked on the floor here?"

"She was crouched in front of the air conditioner and looked asleep. When I touched her to wake her, she fell over, and I saw she was dead— and I don't understand why. She was fine last night."

"You said earlier she was sick."

"Fine meaning she was alive. But she was sick."

"Sick how?"

"To her stomach. When I woke up, the shower was on, so I assumed she was in the shower. She wasn't—she was here."

"What's her full name?"

"Chatterley is all I know. My business partner hired her through a reputable modeling agency." He didn't say that his business partner was his wife. Patton didn't want to bring Tess into this if he could help it.

"Chatterley sounds like a call girl name, eh, Henderson?" said Jimenez.

"Yep. 'Hot Babes to You,'" the hotel man said as if quoting something. Henderson stared at Chatterley.

Patton said, "She's a nice young woman who was going to college, modeling at conventions."

"A model," said Henderson the way someone might say "cunnilingus."

"Yeah, models like to work nights in hotels," said Kelly.

"Shove it," said Patton, jerking toward the guy without thinking.

Jimenez grabbed Patton's arm. "Slow down, buddy. Something you're not telling us?"

"What's that supposed to mean?" said Patton, yanking his arm back.

"A young dead naked girl in your room, and we shouldn't be suspicious?" said Kelly.

"You all are being disrespectful," Patton said. "I didn't know her that well, but she was friendly, and she knew things." As he said it, he was madly running over what things she knew to impress these jerks. "She was training to be a chef. She knew a lot about bread."

The moment it came out of his mouth, he knew it sounded stupid. He wished he was faster on his feet.

"Bread?" said Kelly.

"She had a mind that picked up facts."

Henderson, the hotel guard, laughed.

Officer Kelly said, "We've got it, Henderson. You can go." Henderson nodded as if caught with a dirty magazine. He looked away and left.

"No signs of violence or needle marks so far," said Officer Kelly, and Patton looked over at Chatterley, who was completely exposed again. Unlike Henderson, Kelly was now dispassionate and could have been examining a pound of noodles. Patton couldn't watch any more.

For the next twenty minutes, the officers photographed the scene—not just her body and room but the entire suite—and they asked Patton little. He thought about how Russ at the copy place near his house had died recently. He only knew Russ from the occasional need-it-now photocopy orders he gave the guy. The man had a beard, was no taller than five three, and was now dead, and Patton had felt sad when he heard the news the man had died at fifty from a heart attack. Chatterley was far worse. She was younger and had so much ahead of her.

His eyes started pooling, so he turned away. These jerks wouldn't get more entertainment. Still, just yesterday at the convention, Chatterley had arrived in costume and listened attentively as he'd explained how she'd hand out brochures. She seemed fascinated by his company and his quick tour, and he was impressed by all her questions about beneficial bugs. She projected the sense that his company was more than just a job for her but something really cool.

Toward the end of the day at the convention center, she had skated innocently, even eagerly, toward him, her dark hair bouncing and her funny set of red-bulbed antennae bobbing. Beautiful.

"I think that guy over there wants to talk with you," she'd said.

"Which guy?"

"The guy right behind me who's probably gazing at my tush right now."

Patton had glanced and saw a large man in a black suit indeed admiring her. Patton's eyes automatically fell to the man's badge hung around his neck. A purple badge would mean he was a manufacturer—not helpful. A blue one would mean he was an exhibitor like himself—not helpful. A yellow one meant he was an "industry professional"—not likely helpful unless he was in the media. A red badge, the best, meant he was a buyer, and this man's tag was red. The name of the man's company was one word. "Target," Patton said. He'd been trying to get this man's attention for years. Wayne Jones-Bradbury.

"Yeah, Target," said Chatterley, "The chain store, right?"

"Oh, man," said Patton, "If the Pope were into purchasing, this guy's the Pope."

"Hold it a second," said Chatterley, and she reached for Patton's tie and straightened it, pulling it tighter. The small gesture surprised Patton—something his wife wouldn't have done.

"There," she said. "You're handsome." She smiled. "Go get 'em."

He strode confidently toward the man, his hand outstretched. "Mr. Jones-Bradbury. I'm Patton Burch, the president of BenBugs. I'm glad you found our booth."

"How could I miss it?" said Jones-Bradbury, nodding toward Chatterley. "And now, with everyone interested in a green environment, it's time I took a look at what you do. So ladybugs really eat up the bad critters, do they?"

"They sure do." Patton pointed to a large clear dome bolted onto barstool legs. It was filled with ladybugs walking like moving dots of paint in a terrarium environment of small green leaves.

"Ladybugs sure are cute," said Jones-Bradbury, and they both turned to Chatterley, who gave a big energetic smile. Her oval face had a strong chin with a tiny cleft and high cheekbones that, Patton imagined, photographed beautifully.

Like Daniel Webster fiddling the right music, Patton showed him the point-of-purchase stands and packaging, explained the boxes of beneficial nematodes, the live earthworms, the earthworm castings, the trichogramma, and more. Patton enthusiastically explained how Target could benefit from the Eco-movement and how BenBug was prepared to help. Mr. Bradbury-Jones listened intently, asked questions, and twenty minutes later said he'd like to meet Patton the following week in Los Angeles. He'd been looking for something like this. At that point, the lights overhead blinked, and the P.A. announced it was the end of the day's show.

Tess had been right. Chatterley had paid for herself. Patton figured tens of thousands of dollars in new sales could follow.

A knock on the hotel door now had his attention. Officer Kelly beat him to the door, and when it swung open, a woman dressed well in a beige skirt, white blouse, and dress coat was at the door. She was probably in her late thirties. "Detective Franken," Kelly said. The woman nodded and entered.

While they spoke in soft voices, they each looked at Patton sitting on the couch, and Patton felt chilled, knowing they suspected him. Detective Franken approached him. Patton realized he should call his mother after this. She had a lot of lawyer friends, so she'd know what to do.

"I'm Detective Jill Franken, Homicide."

"Homicide?"

She offered her hand, and Patton shook it. He said, "But isn't this an accident?"

"It's not like she's grandma dying at ninety-five. Detectives are often called even in what may be a natural death. We're trained to help determine the cause. I can use your help. How did the young lady die?"

"I don't know," said Patton, frustrated. "I woke up, the shower was on but she wasn't in it, and I found her in front of the air conditioner already dead."

"Did she take any drugs?"

"Not that I know of."

The detective walked over to Chatterley, once again covered completely by the blanket. She pulled the blanket back, examined Chatterley a moment, and then let the blanket down easily.

"Did you have sex with her?"

"No."

"You sure?"

"Why would you say that?"

"She's naked."

"She fell asleep on top of the bed with her clothes on. That's how I saw her before I went to bed."

"Did she have trouble breathing earlier in the night?"

"Yes. She used an inhaler. She had asthma."

Franken nodded knowingly. "There are drugs in an inhaler. You said no drugs."

"I thought you meant illegal."

"The shower was on, you say?"

Patton nodded.

"I've seen a few asthma deaths. When asthmatic people get desperate in breathing, and they don't have an inhaler that works, the steam in the shower or the cool air of the air conditioner sometimes helps them breathe. Sometimes it's not enough."

"You don't say," said Jimenez, coming from the other room, seemingly irritated.

"It's true. Learned it from a coroner in Philly, and now I have a stepdaughter with asthma. Did you see how she has a blue tint?" She pointed toward the cloaked body for Jimenez's benefit. "That comes from suffocation. Her last moments weren't good ones. Her pulse quickened and she probably grabbed at her throat. Of course, she didn't have food stuck in her throat—it's her bronchi, her airways, that are narrowed, so the Heimlich maneuver wouldn't work. She rushed into the shower." She turned toward Patton. "She'd been in her clothes, you said?"

He nodded.

"Were they important to her?"

"She was in a ladybug costume for our convention," said Patton. "She'd have worn them today."

"People do the darndest things when they're dying," said Franken. "People choking on meat in a restaurant will rush into the rest room to vomit up the suffocating plug because they're too embarrassed to do it in front of fellow dinners. She didn't want your costume wet."

Patton winced as she spoke. He didn't want to know these things.

"Don't go assuming she died from asthma," said Jimenez.

"I know my job, Jimenez," said Franken. "As she gasped for air, the level of carbon dioxide in the blood increased rapidly. It's called hypercarbia, which produces extreme anxiety and creates the blue tint, also called 'cyanotic.'"

She turned and whispered to Patton, "The young turks are always nipping at my heels, trying to move up. They have a lot to catch up on."

Franken turned back to Jimenez. "Her heart, trying to get the oxygen it needed, pumped harder, and she ran in here for the air conditioner. It didn't work. Her efforts to breathe soon came weaker and more shallow. Unconsciousness and death took over."

"Once we're done photographing, we're out of here." Jimenez glared at the detective and returned to the bedroom. A series of light flashes started from the room.

"I'm trying to figure out what might have been the trigger. Do you wear a lot of cologne?"

"No."

"Were you two smoking anything, such as cigarettes, pot, or crack?" she said.

"We didn't smoke anything. I don't smoke. She didn't smoke."

Franken pulled back the blanket on Chatterley's body, pulled on latex gloves, and pulled back Chatterley's arms and fingers, probably sensing for rigor mortis, Patton guessed. The woman examined Chatterley's skin for marks, and looked on her elbows and between her toes, probably for puncture wounds, redoing what Officer Kelly had done. "So I won't find any of your semen in her or on her clothes or sheets? Heavy breathing in sex can be a trigger."

"No," he said. "No sex. I've never wanted to be like my father."

"Your father?"

Patton waved it off. "Not important. He was unfaithful to my mom. With Chatterley, you're making it seem sleazy when it wasn't. No illegal drugs—at least that I saw—no smoking, and no sex. And isn't this a climate best suited for asthma patients?" Patton said. "None of the triggers you mentioned were here."

"Actually, dust in the bedroom and dust in the kitchen are popular triggers. And dust isn't just dust, you know. There're dust mites, fungal spores, human hair, skin flakes, and more. It's the small stuff that can do 'em in."

Patton nodded. This lady knew her stuff.

"Are you married?" she asked.

"Not to her, but—"

"Have you ever had sex outside of your marriage before?"

"Can't you understand?" he said in emphasis. Calm down, he told himself. Was this woman trying to make him upset? If so, she was doing a good job. He said, "No sex. And am I supposed to answer such questions without a lawyer?"

"This is just an interview. You're a witness. You can refuse to talk. You can leave anytime."

"But this is my room."

"I'm not here to arrest you—just talking with you. You have a dead girl in the room here. Can't I help but wonder what happened? Don't you think I should ask you questions?"

"You have a good point."

Jimenez stepped back in with Kelly. "We've catalogued everything. We also checked thoroughly for drugs. No drugs. Do you mind if we go?"

"Yeah, fine," Franken said. The two officers passed Patton, each glaring at him as if he were some perverted killer.

"May I look around now?" Franken asked. "Search the premises some more?"

"I suppose—cooperating, right?" He pointed toward the bedroom.

Patton wasn't sure what he was supposed to do, but he followed. Franken noted the open purse on the floor, and she pointed. "Were you trying to find something in her purse?"

Patton shook his head. "When I woke up, I found it that way."

"You touched nothing? We won't find your fingerprints on anything?"

"Maybe on her purse and inhaler."

"Why's that?"

"I was trying to find out why she died. It didn't make sense. Young people don't just up and die."

The woman nodded. "After you found her dead, what did you do exactly?" Franken had out a notepad.

"This really shook me up. I was …" He paused trying to remember exactly what happened. "I remember I took her pulse just to be sure. I felt nothing—just her cold skin. The air conditioner was still blasting on her, so I turned it off. I thought I should call someone, but should I call the police directly, 911, security or—?" He was going to say "lawyer" but he didn't want to appear he needed a lawyer. Still, he had considered a lawyer, but would he call a criminal lawyer? He didn't know any.

"So you called security. We received a call from Henderson."

Patton remembered glancing around for the room's phone. It was on a glass end-table next to the easy chair. But he hadn't used it right away. He now stared at her in the other room again. She still didn't move, as solid and silent as a bookcase.

"Did you move anything or straighten up after you called the hotel's security man, Henderson?" Franken said.

"I thought she shouldn't be like that, so cold and naked," Patton said. "I came in here and yanked the bedspread off to cover her. I heard a 'bonk' sound and looked back—something had fallen off the bed—but Chatterley needed the bedspread, and so I put it over her first."

"Uh-huh," said Franken, writing quickly.

"Her eyes showed nothing. They didn't reflect anymore. So I closed her eyes. I remember wondering had she taken drugs when maybe she'd been in the bathroom, but she had not seemed drugged at any point—beyond the wine we had at dinner."

"So you had something to drink here?"

"I had a drink and watched TV. She was on the bed. At one point she'd rummaged in her purse and pulled out that blue inhaler." He pointed to the nightstand at the blue object.

CHAPTER 3

"There's no prescription label on it," said Franken. "My stepdaughter has one of these, and there's always a label. In fact, look here. There used to be one."

"I don't know anything about that," said Patton.

"Albuterol, I bet it is," she said.

"All I know was she was able to breathe easily then, calmly. Her breathing was good, but she said she felt sick, so I let her rest on the bed. This morning when I came back in here after I'd covered her, I found the inhaler on the floor. It must have fallen from the bed. I picked it up and placed it on the nightstand."

"And her purse?"

"It was next to the nightstand. I'd looked through it."

"For drugs?"

Patton nodded. "I mean really, why would a young person die? It didn't make sense."

Franken nodded and pulled out a digital camera from her purse. She photographed the purse as it lay open from three different angles. Patton knew Jimenez had been photographing, too, but Franken seemed to want her own angles. She then photographed the bed.

"Why the bed?" asked Patton.

"Scene of the crime."

"There was no crime in the bed."

Franken nodded and knelt next to the contents of the purse on the floor. With her latex-gloved hand, she turned a few things over. There was a compact, a few lipsticks, and all the other stuff. She photographed it. Something seemed to catch Franken's eye and, kneeling on the ground next to the bed, reached for a tan object, her wallet. Patton hadn't seen the wallet.

Franken opened Chatterley's wallet and pulled out a driver's license. "Chatterley Langstrump. Her license says Chatterley Langstrump. You think it's real?"

"Her name or license?" said Patton.

"Probably neither. Maybe that's why there's no prescription label on her inhaler. She took it off because it had her real name."

"She said she went to the College of Southern Nevada, the culinary program."

"We'll check into that." Franken looked further into her wallet and pulled out five one-hundred-dollar bills. "Did you pay her in cash for her services?"

"If you're suggesting sex for hire again, you're wrong. Her company was paid in advance for modeling." He forced himself to pause and then talk more calmly. "I was planning to give her a big tip when it was over, but the convention is still on. As proof by the costume on the floor, she was a ladybug for my booth at the convention."

"Is there someone at the company who can confirm she worked for you at the convention?"

Patton thought of Tess, but he didn't want her to know about this right now. "I'm in town for the Lawn and Garden convention. Everyone will be at our booth at nine. Ask any of them." He glanced at his watch. Nine would be in a just over an hour.

"This is your chance to explain everything," said Franken.

"I explained."

"All right," she said. "Go through exactly what happened last night and how you came to find her this morning. One step at a time. I want to make sure I have this right. I'll write the main parts down, then you can review it for accuracy and sign it." Franken sat with pen poised. Patton went through the whole thing again, and she wrote.

"Any point, no matter how small, you might have left out?"

"One thing: I sensed she was scared of someone or something, which is why I think she felt comfortable here and fell asleep."

"What do you mean?"

He explained how Chatterley and Faith had been talking intently when he first saw them, and how Faith gave Chatterley a key to her place. Why would Chatterley stay in another place if she had her own place? Later she said she hadn't felt like being alone, so maybe she was running away from something or someone.

Franken smiled patiently as if Patton were just like the younger policemen, nipping at her heels.

"I realize her death has to be hard on you, and you're struggling for answers. The answer is usually quite simple, and I already sense this is probably just asthma. I'll check up on a few details here, but it's not as if someone snuck into this room last night and killed her, right? Wouldn't you have heard someone?"

"I'd hope so."

"And that leaves you killing her, or it's an accidental death. What do you want me to think?"

"You asked for unusual details, so I'm giving them to you."

"It's sad when anyone dies from asthma, and it's why I'm vigilant with my stepdaughter."

He nodded.

"Here's my card with my cell phone number at the bottom. Call me if you remember anything else."

He took the card. "So what happens now?"

Franken finished two more sentences before she stopped writing. "May I see your cell phone?"

Patton considered. "Sure. Why?" He gave her his small flip phone.

"Any photos of her in here, kinky or otherwise?"

"Just a couple—normal."

Franken apparently knew what she was doing, and she saw the photo of Chatterley from the elevator. "A nice shot," she said. When she came to the one of Patton and Chatterley together holding each other that Faith had taken, she frowned.

"That photo was taken after a guy punched me for a cab."

She pushed a few more buttons and came up with Patton's call record. Franken wrote the numbers down. "Okay," she said, handing back the phone. "I have your number. What's your home number?"

Patton gave it to her.

"All right. Please read this statement over. If it seems accurate, please sign it, and we're done."

Patton read the one page, which covered his main points in very neat handwriting. He wondered if to be a detective one had to have good handwriting. He signed, and Franken took the paper.

"We'll call you later today most likely," said Franken. "Please keep your phone on. I see it has a good charge."

"Okay. Will you call her parents or whomever?"

"With an accidental death, that'll be the coroner's job. He'll first have to figure out her real identity."

"What if the coroner can't find out?"

"I wouldn't worry about that. I'm just waiting here for the coroner. You can wait with me, or you're free to go until we clear out the room. When you come back, she'll be gone."

"So I don't have to go to headquarters?"

"Nope. Go to your convention if you want. We'll be in touch."

Now he thought again about Tess and gritted his teeth. How to explain a dead girl in his room before she jumped to conclusions? This could be a very big mess.

CHAPTER 4

Back on the convention floor before the doors opened for the day, Patton pulled out the live bugs in their enclosures for their stands. A terrarium held Mason bees, dark blue, which were 120 times better pollinators than honey bees or bumblebees. He screwed down a dome with green lacewings, which looked like small green dragonflies. Patton knocked on its cover to see them move. Lacewings did even more than ladybugs, chewing aphids, mealybugs, mites and more.

Did all these bugs see him as their God, giving them purpose and life? No, they were like most people, just banging around, looking to eat, work, mate, and call it a life.

"Where's the ladybug?" asked Ronald Belcraft, the man in charge of BenBugs's shipping, who'd approached him from behind. At first, Patton thought he'd meant the ladybug dome, which he hadn't pulled out yet, but then he realized Ronald meant Chatterley.

"She won't be coming in today," said Patton.

"That's too bad. She really drew the people in. Is someone else taking her place?"

"No. Unfortuately, no."

"She's gorgeous. We should have her back." Ronald wiggled his eyebrows as if this would change Patton's mind. The man's goatee always appeared as if he'd been giving head to a half gallon of chocolate ice-cream. It just spilled around his mouth.

Patton was about to explain about Chatterley when his cell phone rang. It was his mother returning his call.

"Excuse me a moment," said Patton. Stepping away, he said, "Hello, Mom."

"Where are you?" she said.

"I'm in Las Vegas at a convention."

"Gambling is a sure way to lose a lot of money."

"I'm not gambling, Mom. I'm at a convention. I'm on the floor."

"If you have to gamble, blackjack has the best odds."

He heard her exhale the way she did when smoking, which she shouldn't be doing. She had told her doctor and him that she'd stopped. Normally, he'd say something, but he had more important matters.

"Mom, I called you to get a number."

"Your nephew called me," she said.

"Really? What did Fisher want?"

"To wish me a happy birthday."

His mother's birthday was a day after his. Sure enough, he'd forgotten to send her something.

"Happy Birthday, Mom. I'd have called you later after I was off the floor and—"

"Fisher's a good child, you have to admit. It's not too late for you and Tess."

"I can't get into this discussion again. I'm at a convention, Mom. I've told you."

"You act like I'm entering dementia. Is that what you think?"

"No, but you'll next tell me that childlessness is selfish, and I'm ignoring Tess's biological clock—but she doesn't hear it ticking."

"If everyone were like you, you'd have no one to sell bugs to."

"I didn't call you for this, Mom. Maybe we'll have kids, who knows? We're just busy now."

"Too busy for kids?"

"I need to know the name and phone of Dad's partner's son, the criminal lawyer. He always sat with me at the kids table when we were young at those Thanksgiving parties."

"Brian Feinberg?" she asked.

"Yes, that's him. Brian. I could remember his hair, but not his name."

"Why?"

"A woman who was helping us out at the convention yesterday died last night—apparently from asthma, and I was the last person she saw. The police were questioning me."

"You'd better get a lawyer to be safe."

"That's what I was thinking."

"I like Brian."

She had to go into to her home office to look up Brian's number. Her

Pasadena home overlooked the Rose Bowl. As a kid growing up in it, he'd thought of it just as a dark old house, but nowadays tourists in the know photographed it because it had been designed by a famous set of architects, brothers Charles and Henry Greene.

"I've got it," she said. "He's in West Los Angeles," and she rattled off the numbers. Patton thanked her and then asked, "How is Fisher doing?" Fisher was a sophomore in a physics program at UC Berkeley.

"He's studying hard and has a girlfriend. He sounded more upbeat than your wife."

"She called, too?"

"Why wouldn't she? She remembered my birthday. Tess said you and she have some big deal in the works, but she didn't sound happy. She didn't mention the girl who died."

"Did Tess happen to say where she was?"

"You don't know where she is?"

"I'm in our booth, and she's elsewhere—like always." He tried to make it seem no big deal. "Just wondering if she's coming to the booth today."

"You can't call her?"

"I get her voice mail. Maybe her cell's out of juice."

"It's not my place to ask about your marriage, but maybe her biological clock is roaring. You should take her on a special vacation to Venice, Italy. Those Italians know how to live."

Patton squeezed a hand into a ball. "Mom," said Patton. "Can we talk later?"

"You're always avoiding things. Why can't we talk now?"

"Because I'm on the convention floor."

"Love you, too, dear," she said, and he hung up.

— ✺ —

After the call, and with no attendees in their booth at the moment, Patton gathered his employees and told them of Chatterley's death from asthma.

"Did working here cause that?" said Charlene right away. Charlene normally staffed the front as the receptionist. She looked older than her years, big cheekbones and gray hair like a Czech grandmother, even though she was only in her mid-forties.

"I don't know," said Patton. "I was told plain old dust could do it, but the coroner is still investigating the specifics. We shouldn't feel bad that she worked here. She knew her condition better than we did."

"An asthma death in this climate?" said Ronald, incredulous.

"The desert can blow a lot of dust I guess," said Patton. "I'm still shocked, though. She was so young."

"She was a good kid," said Arvid, his main salesperson. "Not what you think a model is like. She was friendly." Arvid was bald because his hair had never grown back after a cycle of chemotherapy to treat lung cancer. The cancer was in remission. The cancer, Patton realized, was just another example of being on the edge of disaster. How did he not fear waking up? Could today be the day?

"Asthma is like a time bomb," said Arvid.

And cancer's not? thought Patton.

"She had her whole future," said Ronald.

They all nodded in tandem. Patton didn't know what to say. They all had their futures, didn't they? They chatted a little more, and then people entered the booth. "All right. Back to work," said Patton, and he tried to smile even if the darkness of the day pulled him down.

At the next break, Patton made the call.

"Law offices," said a cheery female voice.

"Brian Feinberg, please. This is Westie Burch's son, Patton."

"Please hold a moment," she said. He then listened to a violin version of what he thought was a Bruce Springsteen song. Brian Feinberg was just a year younger than Patton and had gone to Stanford for English and moved into law. Patton remembered him as being driven—and also having a good, thick head of dark hair. Patton wished his own hair were so thick. Patton continued waiting to the stringed music. Yes, the song was definitely "Backstreets."

"Hey, Patton," came Brian's voice. "Is everything fine with your mother?"

"Yes, she's doing great—smoking when she shouldn't be, but otherwise well."

"It's been months since I spoke with Westie. Give her my best. What's up?"

He explained who Chatterley was, her death, her fake name, the police and Detective Franken—and the fact that Chatterley was found nude in front of the air conditioner in his room.

"Were you read your rights?" Brian asked.

"No. They weren't arresting me but just interviewing me as a witness."

"I don't understand what this model was doing in your room—or was she a prostitute, is that what you're saying?"

"No, no, an employee who'd been scared about something." He explained Chatterley's intense discussion with Faith at the restaurant and how Chatterley planned to stay away from her apartment by going to Faith's.

"What's that have to do with anything?" said Brian.

"I don't know. Nothing, maybe."

"You're rattled is all. Let me take care of things. It'll all revolve around this young lady's cause of death. If it's asthma, you won't hear from the police again."

"What am I supposed to do?"

"Hang tight. I'll make some preliminary inquiries and assess the situation. Hopefully this'll all go away. It could take days for the coroner to find the cause of death unless they make it a rush job."

"What if they can't find who she was? The clues might go cold."

"Clues? What clues?"

"That's what they say on 48 Hours—that clues start getting cold. The first forty-eight hours are the most critical."

"Are you suggesting this is murder?"

"Why was she scared of something and avoided her apartment?"

"Leave it alone. The police will do their job."

"I feel bad for Chatterley," said Patton. "It doesn't even sound like they'll find out who she really was. Her parents will never know their daughter died. What if no one claims her body?"

"She'll probably be cremated by the state."

"Left as ashes on a shelf?"

"Listen. It's deeply awkward she spent the night with you and died. My recommendation is don't monkey with this. Let the professionals do their work."

"I guess."

"Are you married?" asked Brian.

"Yes. I am. Why?"

"Just curious what you'll tell your wife. Or have you told her?"

"No, I haven't."

"If there's the least suspicion of homicide, the police might assume you had sex and killed her to cover your tracks from your wife."

Patton paused, trying to absorb this. "I still don't know what to tell my wife."

Brian brought up the cost of his services as if to bring up the reality of the situation more. Brian added, "If the coroner calls it an accidental death and the police don't want to pursue it anymore, this will all just go away. You don't know why this young woman changed her name or stayed away from her apartment. Leave well enough alone."

CHAPTER 4

The morning at the convention proved to be busy, but not as many people asked for information as the day before with Chatterley. With each person he spoke to, Patton felt as if it all meant nothing. We were all just imperfect chemistry sets—made from wayward atoms from a lost sun. Then we were gone, to be what next? Ashes on a shelf?

At noon, he pulled Ronald aside. "I need a favor. I have to leave the convention for a while."

"For a meeting?"

Patton nodded. That was as good a reason as any.

What Patton really needed to do was see if he could switch rooms back at the hotel. He didn't want to be in the same room where Chatterley died. He also realized, with a new room, he could tell his wife that Chatterley died in another room. He wouldn't be lying.

Still, he needed to tell Tess about what really happened. It could easily hit the papers or come out some other way. Best she heard it from him.

Ronald agreed to cover the booth, so Patton took off. At the hotel, he asked the front desk clerk if he could switch rooms.

"Was it uncomfortable?" the young man with round glasses asked.

"We had a problem this morning," said Patton. "Room 1012?"

"Oh," the man said, instantly understanding. "Excuse me a moment." He left and returned with the manager, a short older man with blond hair and black roots like an old entertainer. The man happily gave him a new room and even offered to move his suitcase and possessions so Patton wouldn't have to go back into the old room.

With that out of the way, Patton needed to return to the convention center. To be faster, he'd park at the convention center in the same structure that Chatterley had parked her car the day before. He pulled out his van's keys. They looked strange, three keys and a black keyless remote on an impersonal silver ring. It took him a moment to realize they were Chatterley's keys to her Kia and perhaps her apartment. He dropped them as if they were a thousand degrees. He picked them up, glancing back to the front desk to see if the clerk noticed. The man was helping another guest.

Patton again gazed at the keys, contemplating what he should do. Why hadn't he remembered to tell the police? Would they now think he was covering up something? Should he throw them away and let the hotel or police figure out what to do with the car? Even if the police found her real identity soon, it still might be weeks for Chatterley's surviving family to figure out where her car went. He'd call Brian for help with this.

What about that book that Chatterley didn't want him to see? No one knew about the car, so a quick look would mean nothing.

Patton walked out of the hotel and straight to Chatterley's blue car, which seemed to him forlorn now that it didn't have a live owner. He pressed the button marked "unlock" on the keyless remote, and all four doors unlocked. As he pocketed the keys, he must have inadvertently touched the red panic button on the back because the car started honking and its lights flashed. Patton's heart took a leap, and he saw another man a few cars down turn his head to see. Patton yanked out the keys and pressed "unlock" again, and the car fell silent. Patton shrugged at the man who'd watched, and the man yelled, "Happens to me all the time, too."

Patton entered the back and reached under the driver's seat. He pulled out the book. It had the title Lady Chatterley's Lover by D. H. Lawrence. It was a new and expensive leather-bound edition. She'd called it "insurance." What? A lump of some sort held open pages in the middle of the book. The lump was a flattened and not-quite-desiccated yellow rose.

He flipped to the front of the book where there was a short, hand-written note that said, "I'll call you soon. Maybe we can have dinner Tuesday." It was signed "LCL," with a date of three days earlier.

Tuesday night—last night? Was she supposed to meet this guy last night? If so, she hadn't. Was that why she was at the restaurant—waiting for him? Or had she been there to stay away from him? Patton bet the latter. That made sense. Was she going to use the book as some sort of proof in a restraining order? Or was it possible that Chatterley was an escort as the police had said, and she'd use the book to blackmail him? His mind swirled. What if she'd used the day to drum up more clients? This town had so many escort services, seemingly legal, that his car's windshield would get business cards with nearly naked women promising pleasure and in-hotel service. Young men, mostly Mexican, passed out such cards openly on the streets. Even trucks pulled giant billboards of one scantily clad woman or another down the strip with a phone number. With so much competition, maybe Chatterley had been passing out her own cards at the convention, meeting her future customers directly. But he hadn't seen any such cards in her purse or elsewhere.

No. He had to believe in certain truths about people, and Chatterley was a model, not an escort. An escort wouldn't waste her day in a ladybug costume for a mere $300. She didn't come up to his room to make more money. While there'd been an attraction on both their parts, they hadn't acted on it. Now she was dead from asthma.

"LCL"—that could be someone's initials, but more likely it was "Lady Chatterley's Lover." Was this guy a former lover? Probably—and it was understandable how someone could be smitten with her.

Patton put the book on the back seat to pick up its envelope. He saw it had been addressed to "Chatterley Langstrump" with no address. The package must have been dropped off. However, there were a few bills beneath the large envelope showing an address on South Jones Boulevard. The postmarks on the bills were from two days ago.

At that moment, a police siren was approaching, getting louder. He looked out onto Paradise Road and saw the red flashing lights atop a black-and-white, which was racing toward the hotel. It might be for him. He tossed the book and bills back in, slammed the Kia's door and raced toward his van. He leapt in, closed the door, and crouched down. The siren wailed past. It was going elsewhere.

With his heart racing near a thousand, he decided that was it. He wasn't getting involved anymore. He had plenty to do at the convention center, and he needed to get Chatterley behind him. He called Brian again, then and there, and when the receptionist said he'd stepped out and would he like his voice mail, he said yes. He left as a message, "This is Patton again. I forgot to mention I found Chatterley's car keys. Her car is in the parking lot. I'll leave the keys with the hotel manager. Can you call the detective to tell her about Chatterley's car and have it moved? The hotel otherwise will tow it away at some point. It's a blue Kia. Also, I'm hoping they can find her identity through the car's registration. Then her family can be told. That should do it. Thanks."

Patton was done—except for the small matter explaining this to his wife.

CHAPTER 5

The rest of the afternoon in the BenBugs booth was full of people, even without Chatterley to draw buyers. Many shoppers remembered her from the day before. "Hey, where's the ladybug lady? She's hot. She can come eat my aphids anytime."

His group worked particularly hard all day—maybe they felt as bad as he did and stayed focused to not think about things. Tess months ago had bought them all tickets for that night to see Cirque du Soleil's O at the Bellagio for a mid-convention treat. "How about we meet earlier than planned at the Belagio? said Patton, "and I'll take you all to their exceptional buffet?"

"All right!" said Arvid, and the others loved it, too. They just had to change, so they'd meet in the hotel lobby in forty-five minutes.

The buffet was elegant in terms of Vegas, with such top food as venison and Kobe beef, and his group clearly enjoyed it. Still, Patton felt as if he were in a slow set of subtitles in a foreign movie. He didn't react to people's statements right away. He had to process them, and then pretend to be amused after someone said something funny. He kept going back to thoughts of Chatterley dead. She'd been young, alive, happy, and then no more.

Charlene said, "Don't you agree, Patton?" Charlene looked at him for approval, a crab leg in one hand.

Patton was bewildered. "I'm sorry," he said.

"That life's just not fair sometimes. Why should a sweet girl like Chatterley up and die? I wonder why she didn't call 911 if she couldn't breathe?"

"If you can't breathe, you can't talk," said Arvid.

"The system gives them your address," said Charlene. "They'll just come."

"I spoke to the police this morning," said Patton. "Apparently if you're desperate for breath, you're just trying to find a way to breathe, like sticking your head in the cool air of an air conditioner. She was found in front of the air conditioner."

"If she had asthma," Arvid said, "you'd think she'd have one of those breathing things."

"She did," said Patton. "It was out of medicine."

"Poor girl," said Charlene.

After dinner, Patton turned to Ronald. "I'm not feeling so good."

"You didn't eat much," said Ronald.

"I have a headache."

"Are you saying you're not going to O?"

"No. I'm throbbing," said Patton. He handed his ticket to Ronald. "You might be able to sell it to the box office or scalp it. Use the money for yourself."

"Or maybe me or Arvid could get a date," said Ronald, grinning. Patton never spoke to them about their romantic preferences or their love lives. He thought of them like characters on the old Andy Griffith show, where all the men were innocuous bachelors.

As he arrived at the hotel, the shadows were long, and the sun would set soon. After Patton parked, he noticed Chatterley's car still there. God damn it, why hadn't the police moved it? They had all day for this. As he walked near her Kia, he saw something sparkly on the ground, like parts of a necklace, but it didn't register what it was until he walked closer. A broken window. The Kia's rear window was smashed and open. He rushed to the broken window, peered inside, and saw more glass. He'd left the book on the back seat in plain sight. The book and the bills were now gone. Had the book been valuable? He doubted it, but his own car had been broken into once for his Day Timer, his new daily planner worth nothing to someone hoping to sell it. His head throbbed more. Nevermind. This wasn't his concern. If he never had to deal with the police again, that would be fine. He walked, numb, into the hotel.

Nonetheless, the police's ineptness ate at him. Would Chatterley's family ever learn her fate?

He went to the front desk and saw that Chatterley's keys were still in the manager's cubby where the clerk had left them. That clerk was gone. Should he borrow them back? He couldn't do it. The smart thing was to call Detective Franken, he decided. Maybe Brian had forgotten to call. After Patton used the number on her card, voice mail came on immediately: "This is Detective Franken. Leave a message at the beep."

Beep.

"Hello, Detective. This is Patton Burch. We met this morning in regards to Chatterley's death. My lawyer, Brian Feinberg, was supposed to call you, but in case he didn't, I'd found Chatterley's car keys in my pocket earlier. I'd driven her car last night from the convention center to here. Her car, a Blue Kia, is in the hotel's parking lot out front, and I saw just now that its side window was smashed. Someone broke in. Maybe you can find her identity through her car registration and—"Another beep cut him off. Should he call back and say more? Maybe he'd said too much. He was starting to sound like one of the Columbo suspects telling the police how to do their job.

— ❀ —

As he approached his new room, he'd hoped the hotel had transferred everything as planned. When he stood in front of his door, he thought he heard classical music inside. He looked at his envelope for the key. Room 1122. The door, too, had the number 1122. Placing his ear against the door, he heard the music more clearly from inside. Perhaps it wasn't his room. He swiped the key in the door, and the light on the lock went from red to green. He opened the door.

It was a far larger room than his previous one. In fact, it had a marble-topped bar right next to a floor-to-ceiling window that overlooked the pool below, the convention center a few blocks away, and the elevated monorail line on Paradise Road. At the bar, artfully posed with one arm on the marble counter, the other holding a pink Cosmopolitan martini in a martini glass, Tess grinned widely. After fifteen years of marriage, she still carried herself well. Her blond hair, parted slightly left of middle, swung down to shoulder length and shown as brightly as on a shampoo commercial. Her white blouse, body fitting, accented her curves. "Happy to see me?"

"What're you doing here?" he said.

"The deal's done. I thought we'd celebrate after O." She checked her watch. "You didn't go?"

"No."

"So we can celebrate now."

"The deal?"

"You can't be that tired."

"No. I'm just—"

"You're not happy to see me?"

CHAPTER 5

"Very happy." He could throw up, but he stepped over to Tess and kissed her on the lips. When he'd met her in college, she had dark hair. For the past decade, she'd colored it blond. She pulled him close and kissed him fervently—in a way she hadn't done in years. He tried to respond as best he could.

She looked at him closely, puzzled. "I can tell something's wrong."

"No, listen. You look … ravishing, and it's— Give me a few moments to decompress." He moved to a high-backed black leather couch nearby and fell against its embrace. The whole room was modern, all black and white.

She nodded. "I'm sorry. You've been on the floor all day. I was just— I'm happy for us. You got Target going, and Birnam gave us our money."

"What do you mean he gave us money? I thought it was at least a week off."

"He had business in Europe, and so he closed the deal early with a wire transfer."

"On our terms?"

"Yeah."

"I wonder why he was suddenly so eager?"

"He shares in the profits. It's a good deal … Don't you trust me?"

"We have the money?"

"Supposedly. A pile of it, with a credit line to more. That's why I'm celebrating."

He considered and nodded. "It's really going well," he said.

"Why don't you look happy?" she said, "Sometimes I don't get you. A woman on the radio today was saying it's a man thing. Men can't show their feelings."

"That's ridiculous."

"It's not. Boys early on are told not to cry. You're supposed to hold your feelings in and not express them."

"Just the bad feelings."

"I'm not seeing the good ones here. The woman said that by the time boys are men, the feeling-and-empathy thing has atrophied."

"I've never been a fan of talk radio."

"I'm just saying." She looked at him in a friendly way, lifting up her shoulders, holding her hands out. Maybe it was an opening that she'd listen.

"There's one thing," he said.

"One thing?"

He glanced at her briefly then looked at his hands, the very hands that had caressed Chatterley only the night before. "That young girl you hired for the ladybug outfit. She was found dead today." He looked up into Tess's eyes.

"Oh, my God. That's horrible. Oh, you must feel so bad." She came over and sat next to him, put her arm around him. She was better at empathy than he was.

"What happened?" she asked.

"Asthma complications—or so the police seem to think." He stared off.

"Asthma? How terrible. I'm sorry."

"Yeah."

"What a way to go." She looked him in the eyes. "They're not trying to blame us, are they?"

His heart jolted. "Why would you say that?"

"We have those bees. She didn't get stung, did she?"

He sighed. "No. Asthma isn't the same as a bee sting. Besides, the bees can't get out."

"Good." She twisted back to a comfortable position. "That's sad, though, isn't it?"

"Very."

"Maybe I can take your mind off of things." She walked to her suitcase, unzipped the front pouch, and pulled out a sheer negligee. "I stopped at Victoria's Secret the other day." Maybe his mother was right, and her biological clock was roaring.

Behind her, the sky outside was a vast nothingness. "The police had to speak to me, too."

"That couldn't have been fun." She sat next to him and placed an arm around him again. This seemed so unusual for her. "Maybe we should use the nightie now?"

He patted her thigh and stood, saying, "That's a good idea. Let me make a gimlet or something, see if I can catch up to you."

"I've hardly drunk anything."

"I can use one."

He walked to the bar. Behind it, he found clean glasses and an array of mini-bottles of liquor in a display. Each mini-bottle surely was expensive, but that's part of being in a hotel. He selected gin as well as a mini-bottle of Rose's lime juice. He opened the ice bucket on the counter and found Tess had already stocked it with ice. Tess on the couch seemed to watch him carefully.

"What was her name?"

"Chatterley. Seemed like a nice girl."

"Lady Chatterley's Lover."

"What?"

"That's the only place I've heard that name."

"Right. The book…She brought in a lot of business for us—including the guy from Target."

Tess nodded. "I knew a girl in college on my floor of the dorm who died from asthma. I saw her go out in a body bag."

"Body bags for us all someday."

"That's morbid."

"That's the hard thing about having kids, too—knowing that they'll die someday. Must be hard if they go before you."

The puzzlement on her face said everything.

"I'm sorry," he said and poured the lime juice on top of the gin and ice in a lowball glass. "How about I take you out to dinner?"

"You don't want room service?" She held out her hands.

"Room service, absolutely."

She stepped over to him at the bar. "Maybe we can re-create the last party," she said, "and I'm sorry that lately we haven't been more intimate."

"The menopause thing, I thought."

"I saw a doctor last week about it."

"You didn't tell me."

"She said I'm far from menopause. She said, too, a woman's sexual drive increases as she gets older."

"So you're now interested because you're supposed to be?"

She frowned. "That's not a nice thing to say. I've always been interested. You just keep turning me away—except after that party a couple weeks ago."

"Me?" No, that's not right, he thought. He always had desire—and he loved her.

"Yes, like even now," she said.

"That's not fair. Today was just—"

"No, every time I try to initiate, you seem to be tired or something."

"We just have busy lives."

"Maybe you're mostly done with it. The doctor said a man's sex drive diminishes significantly as he ages."

"My sex drive is perfectly healthy," he said with perhaps too much emphasis.

"How can you say that?" Then she paused like someone trying to read the fine print. "Why're you so upset about this girl, anyway?"

"I can't be upset about someone who died? I saw her alive only yesterday."

"Where'd she die? How'd you find out?"

He paused. Maybe too long. "She died in this hotel. Another room."

"I thought she lived in Vegas."

They stared at each other. Was she suspicious? He said, "I went to the Envy steakhouse as you had suggested."

"So?"

"I ran into her there."

"What're you saying?"

"Nothing happened—not the way you're thinking." He continued on, explained the fight for the cab, the dinner, the happenstance of it all. "I wasn't out looking for a dinner or anything. It just happened." He did not go into details.

"Just dinner?"

"Yes, but afterwards she was feeling sick, so I brought her here—just to make sure she'd be okay." He paused to show his good intentions.

"So what happened?"

"I found her dead."

"How many hours are we talking about?"

"In the morning."

She leaned forward and whispered, "You slept with her, didn't you?"

"I didn't sleep with her. I'm not my dad."

"You and your dad! You never told your mother, did you?" When Patton was a teenager, he'd been riding his ten-speed down Orange Grove Boulevard when he happened to notice his father driving a strange blue Volvo, a young blond woman to his side. An hour later, he happened to see the same car parked in a motel across from Pasadena City College where he was taking a class. Weeks later, the same car was there, and this time, he saw his father emerge from a room. "No, I never told my mother because I could never be sure."

"Right," she said sarcastically.

"And why would I tell her now? That's an insane thing to suggest."

"It shows you can keep secrets and mislead."

"Chatterley spent the night because she'd been feeling sick."

"You look so damn guilty, Patton. How am I to take it?"

"I feel bad she's dead."

"Are you saying she spent the night, no sex? You can be like Bill Clinton and say, 'I had no sex with that woman'?"

"No blow jobs, either. Be sensitive. She died of asthma."

She just stared at him.

"She used an inhaler a couple of times." He then described everything as he had to the police. Tess didn't ask about anything. She was just listening, staring at the floor. What was she thinking? His talking, though, helped.

When he was done, Tess walked to the corner of the room where her bag stood. She extended its handle for rolling it. "I don't believe you," she said.

Her cell phone rang, and she reached inside her purse and pulled it out. "Hello?" she barked, then her face changed immediately to surprise. Slowly a smile came on. "Oh? What kind of problem?" She listened and replied, "Listen, I'm happy to help. May I call you back in a few minutes? I'm just ending a meeting."

Patton shook his head. Is that what this was, a meeting? And who was she talking to? What kind of problem?'

She pressed the hang-up button and looked hard at Patton as she walked toward the door.

"Who was that?" he asked. "And what kind of problem?"

"Business. Our business. Anton Birnam if you must know. It's a small problem with the wire transfer that I can handle. That doesn't change our problem here. I can't believe you did this to us, right after we're funded. You're fucking everything up."

"I did nothing wrong. A woman's asthma is not our problem."

"Oh, right," she said, again with sarcasm.

"You know me. I'm not the player type."

"You didn't think," she said.

"I was true to you. This isn't to say that if you and I made—" He left the rest in the air.

"Fucked more? Believe me, I'm about to start, but in ways you might not like."

"And you're perfect?"

"I don't cheat."

"I don't either."

"The good news is I want our company to succeed right now, and bad press about you in the paper or your arrest won't help anything. You better hope this stays quiet, or I'm going to take you for everything you're worth. Maybe this is going to be my company alone."

He held his tongue because he knew she was just blowing steam.

She then strolled calmly to the door, wheeling her bag behind her, and walked out. He thought of running after her, but he knew it'd do no good.

"God damn it." He should just….

He didn't know what he should just do. Maybe go after her, after all. He was reminded of when they first started dating, nothing official, nothing serious, and he was at Gladstone's 4 Fish, a great restaurant on the Santa Monica beach where you'd throw your peanut shells on the floor while you drank your beer and waited for the Surf N' Turf. He was laughing with a tall girl he'd met there in a French tee. God, the woman was pretty, red hair and a husky voice, and when she went to the bathroom, Tess stood suddenly before him, upset. "You act like you're nice, but you're not," she blurted.

"Tess, Tess, what're you doing here?" he'd said, but she didn't answer.

Her face fell like one of those glacier walls in Alaska that snap off and jackknife into the bay. She turned and ran out. No one had ever been that smitten with him before. Right then and there he knew she was the one. He ran after her. He should run after her now.

When he hurried into the hallway, a woman laughed sexily, and he stopped. Tess? A couple in their thirties kissed passionately against the next room's door, he in a tux, she in a dusty rose bridesmaid's gown. The man's key-card fell from his hand as he fondled the woman's breasts.

The woman pulled back, glaring at Patton. "This isn't a show. What you want's uptown."

"No, I was just—" What was the point in explaining?

When he got to the elevators, Tess wasn't there. The doors opened, and a lone girl about ten was in it with a towel wrapped around her pink bathing suit. He moved in quickly. Tess couldn't have gotten too far, he thought.

As the elevator moved down, the girl pressed a bottom button repeatedly as if to the mantra, "Stranger danger." To reassure her, he said, "Swimming's always fun when it's so hot."

She pushed the button harder.

The doors opened, and she bolted out. He rushed out, too, and when the doors shut, he realized he wasn't in the lobby but the floor above. The little girl ran quickly down the hall, glancing back at him as she lurched around the corner.

As he hurried down the grand staircase, the picture windows before him revealed Tess pushing into a yellow cab. "Hey," he shouted though he knew it'd do no good. As he sped down, the cab took off. Where was she going? To another hotel? To the airport? To a bar?

He stopped at the edge of the parking lot. Nothing seemed to work in this world.

CHAPTER 5

As he stared off at the disappearing taxi, light glinted off broken glass. It was the glass on the asphalt next to Chatterley's car.

Chatterley. He stared at the car and the glass. Why couldn't the damn cops do anything about her car? Would they ever find out anything about her? He imagined the hotel calling to have the car hauled away, and it'd be weeks if ever the police figured out she had a car.

That did it. He couldn't stand this place, this hotel. He sped off in his van, no destination. The sun dipped below the horizon, and everything was getting darker, fucked.

CHAPTER 6

Patton didn't gamble or drink much, so a casino or bar was out. He wasn't hungry or thirsty. Just driving was fine. After a short while on the big boulevard, he noticed a sign for the College of Southern Nevada— now that was interesting. It was Chatterley's college. It was an odd coincidence, he realized, but then again, he probably passed this place before, and the college name hadn't meant anything to him then.

He turned onto Community College Drive. In the dusk, the College of Southern Nevada's parking lot and sidewalk lights flickered on, showing an open and modern campus with pristine concrete-and-glass buildings, some of them festooned with large tile, some round, some square, and some of them in bright colors, yellow, pink, and blue. So this was where Chatterley had been going to college.

He took a left at the next street. A street sign showed Jones Boulevard. Her address from the bills was on South Jones Boulevard, and it made sense to have an apartment near the college. If the police never found her identity or address, the apartment she had would be packed up and maybe the contents sold. That sucked. The numbers on a nearby building showed her apartment was near. He parked, wanting to see where Chatterley had actually lived. If no one else cared about her, he did.

The dusky light revealed a complex of small two-story white stucco buildings with red-tiled roofs. Some of the windows arched elegantly, in contrast to the other plain square aluminum windows. The lights along the concrete pathways highlighted palm and pine trees standing on a mostly brown lawn. The hedges had been clipped clumsily and looked lopsided. The complex as a whole looked well laid-out and built, but it was kept on the cheap. A sign for the complex said, "La Jolla Beach Apartment Homes—2 Bedroom/2 Bath." Where was the beach? At best, there would be a pool.

He got out and walked, scanning for her exact apartment. Did she have a roommate? She hadn't said, but he guessed not. When he found her building, he looked on the mailboxes and saw "Langstrump" as the lone name for unit 3. He looked around to see if anyone was watching. This would be awkward to explain to police why he was here, but she wasn't a priority for the police. He might be the only person who cared for her.

Her apartment was on the bottom floor. Two tall rose bushes stood on either side on her porch, but many of the leaves were yellowed and had holes. That and browning flower buds told him there were aphid problems.

A solitary black ceramic poodle by the front door stood guard. He tried her door. It was locked. He stared at the door knob then. His fingerprints were now on it. Shit. He polished the knob with his shirt. With a homicide detective on the case, it was worth being a little paranoid.

The window by the front door had a curtain, so he couldn't see the inside. This was where she'd lived, though. He sighed. She'd never see any of this again.

He stepped across the crunchy grass away from the building and to the side to get a better sense of the place. A light flicked on in the upstairs apartment, and a young woman in a t-shirt and shorts walked past her bed to pull down her shade. Directly below, then, had to be Chatterley's bedroom. Chatterley's bedroom window was open. With the heat of Las Vegas, why would a window ever be open?

He moved closer. A quilted bedspread covered her neatly made bed, which also held many pillows. Women loved pillows. On one of them, a poodle had been embroidered. She loved poodles. Tess loved cats. The cool air from inside poured onto his face. The air conditioning must have been running constantly. Just below the window was a short bookcase, and the top held glass figurines of animals such as horses, a pig, a penguin, and a poodle, all toppled over. Someone must have crawled in through this window and knocked over the glass.

Patton stepped back, his mind racing. Why would someone break into her place? Was her ex-boyfriend, LCL, a stalker? The young man probably didn't know she was dead and maybe he was getting mad that she wasn't responding. Maybe he'd broken in and was waiting for her. Patton shook his head. His imagination was working overtime, and he was probably reading too much into the situation. Then again, with a false identity, she was hiding from someone.

He returned to the window and spoke, "Hello? Anyone here? Chatterley's dead, so there's nothing to wait for." Nothing. He stood still for minutes and not a single sound came from inside. He heard voices behind him, though, coming down the sidewalk, and he froze. He flashed on Law and Order on other crime shows where bystanders offered important clues. What if these people later picked him out in a lineup, which would be used to convict him wrongly of Chatterley's murder? But he wasn't a suspect. But what if this made him one? This was stupid coming here, and he had to do something. He quickly lifted himself into Chatterley's bedroom and stood back from the window.

His heart raced as he watched two girls in bikinis walk by, carrying towels. The pool must be down that way. He turned, saw someone and almost screamed, but it was his reflection in a mirror. Calm down, calm down, he told himself. This was insane being inside her apartment. Get out.

He was about to do so when a poster of Julia Child on a Time magazine cover caught his attention. The light from the sidewalk illuminated it. An artist's rendering showed Child in her confident fifties, surrounded by a silver-skinned fish, copper pans, and the statement "What's cooking." Chatterley had said she wanted to be a chef. Julia Child probably had been a good inspiration.

Using the flashlight app on his smart phone, he looked at the books in the bookcase under the window. Hardback mysteries by Michael Connelly and Robert Crais filled most of the second shelf, with five Connelly novels stacked on the floor. The top shelf had five cookbooks including the Fannie Farmer. It occurred to him that these were some of her most treasured books and her name might be in them. As he reached for a cookbook, he pulled his hand back. His fingerprints would do damage if the homicide detective found any reason Chatterley's death was suspicious. Yes, she died of asthma most likely and nothing probably would happen beyond that, but he should take precautions.

It was for that reason he went into the kitchen to get some small plastic bags for his hands. From the dim sweep of his light, the kitchen looked extremely messy, with every drawer open—odd that a chef wasn't neater. Still, that made it easy to spot yellow rubber dishwashing gloves in a drawer by the sink. He also grabbed a dish cloth.

Back in the bedroom, his hands protected, he used the dishcloth to wipe the windowsill where his fingers and palms had touched to pull himself in. He then opened each of the cookbooks to see if Chatterley's real name were in them. No. The front of the book had a bunch of folded papers, recipes, some handwritten, some printed. The Fannie Farmer Cookbook, which had a blurb on the cover calling it "America's great classic," had bits of paper sticking out, acting as bookmarks. Randomly he chose one marker and found that she'd starred the "Sturdy Soufflé" recipe. That didn't seem like an American classic, though leave it to Americans to turn a delicate delight into something sturdy. Handwriting in the margin noted, "Dad's favorite—good for when he's mad." Chatterley had had an angry father?

At the front of that book, the loose papers weren't recipes but pay stubs from the Blue Oyster Gambling Hall in Las Vegas. That seemed an odd place for paystubs. The name Chatterley Langstrump headed each stub, so he still didn't have her real name. If this casino had been the place that she and Faith had worked together, he now had a way to find Faith.

The address on the stubs showed the casino and hotel on West Charleston, not far from her apartment. He hadn't noticed the casino on the drive over. Much of West Charleston Boulevard was pod malls and small shops for residents, nothing glamorous, nothing for tourists. He pocketed one paystub for the address. He also placed the Connelly books on the floor back onto the shelf, and they filled out the row.

Where might her real name appear? In an address book perhaps? An old-fashioned roll-top desk across the room had letters in its letter holders, pens in a pen jar, and spiral notebooks all over the floor around it. Why was she so messy when her bed was so neat? He swung his light over to her tall bureau, and every drawer was open, underwear and bras, pajamas, scarves, and more hanging out. His mouth fell open. A burglar had been here before him—that's why the window had been open. The burglar had rifled these drawers, the bookcase, the kitchen, and perhaps elsewhere.

On the top of the bureau, an open enameled box caught his attention. He moved his light closer. The jewelry inside her jewelry box looked untouched, including what appeared to be a princess cut engagement ring—a rock on a ring. That was worth something, as were a small group of gold coins next to it. In fact, there was a TV in the corner. What kind of burglar doesn't take the valuable stuff? He'd been after something else.

In the living room, his cell phone and light went out. He had a car charger, but that would take a lot of time. With the kitchen at the back of the apartment, he thought a light from there might not show brightly out front, so he turned it on. That was enough light to see that she had some boxes lined up, partially filled, and surrounded by a big mess of random stuff mostly from the kitchen: pots, pans, jars of spices, canned goods. It appeared as if she was in the opening stage of moving.

That's when the doorbell rang, followed by a hard pounding. Patton dropped to the floor. Should he dash out back through the bedroom window? If it were the police, they'd surely be looking, and it wasn't hard to see that side of the apartment from the front stoop. The hammering repeated. "Chatterley?" a voice said sternly. It wasn't the police. "I see the light on," said the voice.

There was a jangling of keys. Patton pulled off the gloves. He flipped on the light switches by the front door just as the door was opening to a short homunculus of a man.

"What are you doing?" said Patton as if offended.

The man frowned at Patton. "Is Chatterley in?" Balding on top, the man had long, tangled hair on the sides like a goblin. He wore thick wire-rimmed glasses.

"I'm afraid she's not," Patton said, trying to appear as if he belonged there. "May I help you?"

"Who are you?"

"It's none of your business."

"Father?"

"I'm not that old. Are you the manager?"

"No, I'm Tinkerbell the accountant. Of course I'm the manager. She's late on her rent."

"I'm her brother," Patton said, improvising.

"Funny her brothers are popping up all of a sudden. Do you have a book to give her, too?"

That startled Patton. Maybe that had been LCL. "When was my brother here?"

"Earlier. Except he didn't have a key. I wouldn't give him one. He was asking where she was—as if I keep track like Santa Claus."

"What did he look like?"

"You don't know what your brother looks like?"

"I have three."

"Tall, handsome, long dark hair. Mole on his cheek. Know him?"

"Jesse," said Patton, making up a name. He didn't know him.

"He had no mole on his face. Who are you?"

Patton said nothing.

"I'm not stupid," said the manager. "I doubt you or the other guy are her brothers. What's it going to take for me not to see you?"

It took Patton a moment to realize this guy was shaking him down. "You want money?"

"Chatterley's been a horn-of-plenty."

"What?"

"Come now. Like I'm Play-doh? Chatterley has no background that checks out, which is why her rent is so high and why I keep mum."

Patton reached for his wallet. He only had maybe six twenties and some fives. The man watched Patton count. "Did you hit up my brother, too?" Patton asked.

"No. I should've. I will if he shows up again." The man leaned closer, looking impatiently. "Give it all to me," said the man, "and I still need her rent."

"I'll tell her to see you once she gets in."

"Right," he said sarcastically, pocketing the cash and moving off. "Tell her I'm going to change the locks if she doesn't give me the full rent within two days."

The man strode off into the darkness as if he were the baddest manager in town.

Because the manager knew he was there anyway, Patton turned on more lights, sighing. He foresaw the manager fingering him in a lineup. That made finding out Chatterley's real past that much more important if she ever became more than a fading asthma statistic. He put the gloves back on.

In the living room, her walls had three framed landscape photos—one of a desert with blooming orange poppies; another of Paris with the Eiffel Tower, and a third of wind turbines on the water. They didn't particularly look personal—more like what Aaron Brothers Art and Framing sold as standard.

He found nothing useful in the living room and kitchen, so Patton returned to Chatterley's room and her bookcase. Next to the delicate glass animal figures lay two wine corks. One had the word "Kenwood," and the other, "Chateau St. Jean." An empty wine bottle from Chateau St. Jean featured a label with a classical building—the winery, he guessed—and the words "Malbec, 2001, Sonoma County." She knew her wine at dinner, but perhaps these bottles were more than just premium choices. Perhaps some special event was tied to them.

He turned his attention to the roll-top desk. The letters were mainly bills, gas and electric—no phone bills, which could have told a lot. She surely must have had a phone. The long-distance calls would interest him. He looked in the drawers—a few AA batteries, a flashlight, and a long white instrument that looked like a rhino's horn—a dildo. He picked it up. He'd seen women use them on porn sites, but Tess didn't have one as far as he knew. On the bottom was a dial marked "twist for multispeed." He twisted, and it hummed and vibrated. He clicked it off and quickly slipped it back in the drawer and shut it. "I'm sorry," he muttered.

Patton spent several more minutes looking for an address book, but he found none. He had an idea. The manager seemed to know more about her than her own place revealed. Maybe Patton had been too quick not to question him. Patton had a one hundred dollar bill that he kept folded in one of the credit card slots of his wallet for emergencies. Maybe more money would get him more information.

Outside, Patton followed the arrow that pointed the way to the manager. His office and residence was in the second building, and his door was partially ajar. Patton rang the bell. No answer.

Patton pushed open the door. "Hello? Manager?"

He stepped in. A boar's head mounted on a shield-like plaque stared at him from the hardwood floor. The head must have normally resided on the large nail, which stuck out from the wall behind the desk.

Pens, pencils, and shards from a broken ceramic cup were also scattered about. "Mr. Manager?" Patton said.

Patton stepped in farther when he saw all the spattered red paint—no, it was blood, and Patton moved forward. The manager's face—what was left of it—faced the ceiling. His nose, eyes, and mouth had been bashed in to the half cantaloupe that was still his head. Patton grabbed his stomach as he now noticed the boar's snout had blood and brain matter on it. A bathroom door was open nearby, and Patton ran to the room, starting to throw up. Most of it fell into the toilet. The little that didn't, a CSI lab might use to find Patton's errant DNA. Using toilet paper, he cleaned up the rest of his vomit and flushed. With more toilet paper, he erased his fingerprints from the toilet's flusher handle.

When he was done, Patton rinsed out his mouth. His instinct was to run, but his intellect told him to calm down and consider what had happened there. Who did this, and why? Patton guessed he was just a few steps behind whoever had ransacked the apartment. Had the intruder seen me? Patton thought. Am I next?

Moving quickly, Patton made sure he didn't step in any blood.

Peering from a window, he saw no one outside. He walked out as close to a normal pace as possible, making a beeline for his van. Once he was almost there, he heard voices approach, and from the van, he again saw the two girls in bikinis. They slowed when they walked by the manager's place. They each looked in at the door open. Patton had forgotten to close the door.

They called out loudly, "Hank?" Stepping up onto the porch, one of them rang the bell. They both stepped inside. Moments later came the screams. Patton took off quickly, making sure his tires didn't squeal.

CHAPTER 7

Patton sat in the driver's seat of his van in the parking lot of the Blue Oyster Gambling Hall and Hotel, keys in hand, and caught his breath. He'd spotted the casino on Charleston. He hadn't planned to pull in until two police cars racing the other way, lights flashing, screamed toward him—probably on the way to the dead manager.

Patton just wanted to hide out. He didn't think about looking for Faith at first. Should he just return to his hotel as if nothing had happened? His hands trembled. He was reminded of when he had to identify his father, who had been hit by a Brink's truck in downtown Los Angeles. Dad had emerged from between two cars and was hit by the armored vehicle. His mother had been in Spain with a friend at the time. Later, an autopsy revealed Dad had had a heart attack—that perhaps he'd fallen between the two cars. Part of his father's head had been run over, flattened, and while Patton had felt sickened then, his main thought was that his father could no longer be unfaithful.

Where was Tess? She needed to know how much worse things were now. Should he call the police to say he, too, had come upon the dead manager? He'd call Brian. His lawyer would have a sober overview and would recommend the right thing.

Los Angeles was an hour earlier, so it should be just after sunset there. He didn't have Brian's cell number. What if he wasn't working late?

"Law offices," said a male voice.

"Brian Feinberg, please. Or would you have his cell if he's not in? This is Patton Burch with an emergency."

"Patton, this is Brian. What kind of emergency?"

"You're answering your own phone?"

"I do after hours. You're in trouble?"

Patton explained how things hadn't gone well in telling his wife about Chatterley, and he'd just been driving to clear his mind when he stumbled onto Chatterley's community college—then her apartment complex. Curiosity took hold and he looked for her apartment.

"I don't understand," said Brian. "The place should be kryptonite to you. Why would you even think of looking?"

"Haven't you ever felt confused and lost, and then this thing is in front of you? I mean, if you saw a sign for the Grand Canyon in half a mile, wouldn't you go?"

"I'm already cringing," said Brian. "Go on."

Patton explained the open window, the girls in the bikinis, and everything else.

Brian didn't say much beyond "Oh, my God" with each revelation. When it came to finding the manager dead, Brian said, "Shit, Patton. You pull in more bad stuff than fly paper at Marty's Meats."

"I know. What do I do?"

"So the girls who found the manager called the police you think?"

"I'd assume. I was on Charleston when two police cars zoomed by. What do I do?"

"I learned a few things from Franken today," he said.

"I thought lawyers and cops rarely spoke to each other except under duress."

"This isn't law as it is on primetime TV. The police and I dance with each other a little, see where we're at and the kind of energy we need to expend. Franken's expecting it'll be a routine asthma death, and we have to wait for the coroner. I thanked her."

"And now it's not so routine."

"Exactly. I'd have called what you found in Chatterley's apartment a simple burglary except, as you said, valuables weren't taken, and now the manager is dead. Do you have an enemy?"

"Enemy?"

"Someone who really hates you and is going out of his way to get you?"

"Not that I know of. I have an average life."

"Maybe not. I have to think things through, and I'll talk with my partners in the morning."

"So I just wait?"

"I'm guessing I'll call Franken tomorrow on your behalf, and she'll want you to come in. In the meantime, go back to your hotel, do nothing, and go to work in the morning, back to your routine."

"Embrace routine."

"I know it's hard. Just do it, and let me give you my cell number."

Patton took it down and hung up.

In front of him over the entrance, a flashing neon cowgirl rode a bull. "Come inside," the sign blazed. Chatterley's friend Faith, he realized, might be inside.

If he didn't know better, he'd swear some capricious god was toying with him. Then again, sometimes the forces of randomness fit just right. That's what every gambler inside the hall was hoping for.

Patton had parked near the pool. He walked to the entrance marked "Casino and Lounge." Inside, as he walked down a short dark hall that had spotlights on old photos of Wild West gambling halls, the murmur of slot machines, little boops and beeps, sang like a chorus of bad robots. In his previous casino-going experience, jackpot sounds were louder, streams of coins cascading down. Not here.

As he entered the high-ceilinged room, the slots were peopled by older men and women who looked like extras in a Woody Allen movie, living caricatures with sunken eyes and big chins, cigarettes dangling from their lips as they sat on stools and concentrated on the spin. The smell of the smoke hit Patton, the very smell he grew up with from his mother, an odor he hated.

A woman in a teal-colored blouse with a necklace of round glass beads had a pronounced dowager's hump. A short seventy-something man, perhaps her husband, stood next to her with thick glasses and a gray goatee. "Come on, baby," he muttered as the three rows spun. A seven came to a stop, then a cherry, then a watermelon.

"Fudgesicle," said the woman.

"Let's try again," said the man, and Patton felt instantly sad, thinking these people's last heartbeats were being used up here. Then he had a worse thought: maybe he'd be like these people in his later years, newly let out of jail, broken, looking for a little luck, too.

An older cocktail waitress in a short dress whose plunging neckline revealed crescents of two small bowls of flesh said, "Would you two like a drink?"

"A screwdriver each," said the man.

The woman stood and kissed her husband on the cheek as the waitress moved toward Patton. "Thanks, hon," the woman said, and Patton realized that as sad as this place was, these two people had each other.

"Would you like a drink?" asked the cocktail waitress, who now was at his side.

"I'm not gambling," he said.

"You looked like you could use a drink is all, dear," the lady said.

"I'm looking for a waitress named Faith," said Patton.

"Waitresses aren't allowed to mingle, if that's what you're looking to do." The waitress, closer to his mother's age, winked.

"That's not why I'm here." He pulled out Chatterley's pay stub and showed it while covering Chatterley's name. "I'm from accounting and have a question for Faith."

"At this hour?"

"Casinos never sleep," said Patton.

"Her shift starts in, well, what time is it now? They never have clocks in a casino."

Patton glanced at his watch. "Ten-thirty."

"She'll be in in a half hour. You didn't have this information in accounting?"

"No one tells anyone shit around here," he said.

"Ain't that the truth.... I'll get you a drink as you wait for her."

"How about a Heineken? Maybe I'll throw a quarter into a slot and see how my luck is."

She frowned at him. "These machines don't take coins anymore—haven't for years."

"No?"

"You need a debit card from the cashier. You say you work for this company?"

He tried to pawn off an easy laugh. "Shows you how I don't get out of the office much."

She shook her head as she walked off.

In the back at the cashier's cage, a short dumpy man leaned against the counter and stared at Patton. He looked as if he owned the place, even if his long blond hair looked ridiculous and his suit coat strained from probably too many Big Macs. He guessed the man probably had a ridiculous name, too, like Fabio.

The waitress returned with his beer, and he sat in the lounge area where a bearded man at a microphone sang, "Hiding on the back streets, hiding on the back-ack streets." He wore a leather coat and torn t-shirt, looking much like Bruce Springsteen on the Born to Run album cover. This guy was much heavier, though, more like Elvis in the later years. Leave it to Vegas.

Patton walked briskly to the cashier's cage and asked for a ten-dollar debit card. In seeing his wallet empty, he remembered he'd given everything to the manager. He used his emergency hundred-dollar bill he kept folded elsewhere in his wallet. As the rail-thin cashier programmed the card, the blond-haired man that he'd dubbed Fabio earlier moved into the cage with a banded stack of twenties. He handed it to the cashier along with a clipboard to sign. "Excuse me," she told Patton. She signed, then inserted the money into the cash register.

Fabio stared at Patton a moment then stepped away, and the cashier handed Patton his card. "Good luck," she said.

The slots closest to the lounge were not nickel but quarter machines, and you could bet up to five quarters at once. Patton's point wasn't to win but to stay there awhile, so he bet only one quarter at a time. Sometimes he won a few, so it took him twenty-five minutes to reach zero. A new waitress approached—Faith. She wore the same short dress as the older woman earlier, but Faith looked much better in it.

"Another Heineken, sir?" she said, not recognizing him. She held a tray with a few empty glasses and a full Corona bottle.

"Yes, I'd— Hey, I've been waiting for you." He smiled, trying to be casual. Her eyes rolled at the ceiling. She must have heard it every day.

"And what drink would you like?" she said.

"I met you at a steak house with your friend Chatterley yesterday. Your boyfriend came to take you out."

She gazed at him more seriously now, and a smile burst on her face. "I remember, you were a general—Petraeus, was it?"

"Patton."

She snapped her fingers and nodded. "Chatterley's so great, isn't she?"

"Yes," he said. "I have some bad news, though. She died last night."

She stared at him as if trying to figure out if he were serious. "Die? How'd she die?"

"Asthma."

She dropped her tray, and glasses shattered when they hit the carpeting. She knelt down instantly to clean up the mess, and Patton helped her. A bartender started running over, but he stopped abruptly, looking at something behind Patton. Patton turned. Fabio was running toward them.

"I've got it," yelled Faith.

"That's the second time this week," said Fabio, nearby and glaring.

"I'm sorry. Take it out of my pay."

"Damn right I will."

"It was an accident," Patton said, standing. "Give her a break."

"You just go back to playing your single quarters," said the man. The guy knew he'd been playing single quarters?

Once Fabio was away, and Faith had all the broken pieces on her tray, she stood. "How do you know she died?"

"The police interviewed me. I seem to be the last to have seen her."

"Fuck, fuck, fuck," she said shaking her head as if she were partly responsible. "Sometimes she had a problem with all the cigarette smoke here. That's why she finally left. When's her funeral?"

"No telling. The police still need to contact her relatives, but it turns out her name Chatterley isn't her real name."

"I figured that, but in Las Vegas, you don't ask about such things."

"Do you know how to get a hold of her parents or someone?"

Faith shook her head. "I know she hated her dad."

"Where's she from?"

"Back East she said."

"New York? Massachusetts?"

"She never said, and I didn't push it. She always seemed like such a California girl to me, though."

"Her mannerisms, maybe?"

"Something. And she once said she saw Coldplay in San Francisco."

"Coldplay?"

"A band. A popular one."

"Right." San Francisco could work, but it was a big place. "If she were from San Francisco, where would I look there?"

"You're going to find her parents? Really?"

He hadn't meant he would, but her asking brought a new clarity. "I don't get why something bad like this could happen to such a good person. What kind of God lets this happen? Maybe I'm sounding stupid."

"You're sounding nice."

"I feel bad for her parents and friends."

"All I can tell you is she hadn't waitressed much before here. She'd told our boss—" and she shot a thumb toward Fabio in the cashier's cage, "that she'd worked in a fancy bar back East and served a lot of white nuns."

"Religious ladies?"

"The name of a drink. When she was asked what's in it, she didn't know, but he liked her so much she got the job. I helped her learn the ropes. You're right—she was a really good person. When she first started working here, I'd just left my husband. He was a choreographer—cheating on me. I was going to stay in this hotel, but Chatterley took me in, no questions asked. She said she'd been thrown out of her home as a teenager and knew how tough it could be."

"What else do you know about her? Any little thing can help."

She paused a while as if it were an important quiz, then shook her head. "I feel bad I don't know more about her. She didn't talk a lot about herself. She was always asking about me—kind of motherly, you know?"

"Just before I met you, I'd gone into Envy earlier, and I saw you two talking intensely. Was it about a guy coming after her?"

She nodded.

"I knew it," he said. "So what did she tell you?"

"At first I thought she was talking about our boss." She thumbed toward the cashier's cage where Fabio was against the counter again. He looked up, glared, and motioned for her to get going.

"That guy?"

She nodded. "He was always around her. After she quit the casino, he came to me upset, asking if she'd left because of him. I told him no, it was the smoke, but he didn't seem to believe me. The guy is creepy, but she said it wasn't him, so I asked who, and she said a former boyfriend."

"From where?"

"She only said Back East again. She didn't give me his name. The guy was expecting to meet her that night, but she wasn't going to. She told me she'd moved here to get away from him."

"She never told you her real name?"

Faith shook her head. "Anyway, I gave her my key last night so she wouldn't have to go home."

"So she was scared?"

"More like super irritated."

"He'd left a book with her apartment manager who I guess gave it to her."

"She didn't mention it."

"It was like to prove he knew who and where Chatterley was."

"She didn't particularly like her manager, either. He was kinda creepy."

"He died tonight, too. Murdered."

She gaped. "What the hell's going on?"

"I don't know."

"Let me give you my number—so you can tell me when her funeral is if there is one." She waved him to the bar, and he followed. She grabbed a cocktail napkin and quickly scrawled a telephone number and handed it to Patton. "So call me, will you?"

"Gladly," he said. Fabio hurried down the aisle toward Faith. "Now get out of here," she told Patton.

Patton returned to his machine and watched as Fabio quietly voiced

CHAPTER 7

his displeasure at Faith. Fabio turned to glare at Patton, then marched right up.

"Give me that napkin. Our waitresses are not supposed to mingle."

"She's not. She's a friend of a friend."

"He was talking to me about Chatterley," said Faith, coming up.

Hope flashed on the man's face a moment, then he turned mean again. "Come with me outside," he barked at Patton. "And give me that napkin."

Patton stuffed the napkin in his front pocket. He wasn't giving this guy anything.

"Outside." Fabio pointed to a side door on the other side of the lounge marked "Emergency Exit." Was this guy going to fight him for the napkin? As they walked closer to the door, smaller letters said. "Emergency Exit only. Alarm will sound."

"Here?" said Patton. Fabio pushed him hard into the door, which opened to no alarm.

"Hey, what the hell? Aren't there some kind of rules?" Patton yelled. He found himself in a narrow alley next to a dumpster. God damn this guy.

"There're no rules," said Fabio.

"No rules?" said Patton. Patton kicked him hard in the crotch, surprised at his own derring-do. It had worked in the movie Butch Cassidy and the Sundance Kid, and Fabio fell to the ground. "Fuck you," said Patton. "It's my napkin."

Curled into a fetal position, Fabio looked at him with pained amazement like a kid who'd fallen from the merry-go-round on the playground confused by centrifugal force.

"What did you do that for?" the man squeaked. "I can't ask you about Chatterley?"

"I thought you were going to fight me for the napkin."

"I could care less about the napkin."

"Why were you all Mr. Tough Guy with Faith?"

"I have to be a hard-ass for the girls or they won't listen. Some of them are pretty street-wise. You hurt me."

"Sorry, man," said Patton, offering him a hand up. The man waved him off and stood, massaging near his crotch. "I misunderstood," said Patton.

"My name's Sal. Sal Castello."

"Patton."

"Faith said you know Chatterley. How is she?"

"Dead," said Patton, and the man's face crumpled again as if he'd taken another kick.

"How? Why?"

"Asthma."

Sal could only shake his head. He looked near tears. "Like my daughter." And the man started to cry.

"So what's her real name?" asked Patton, astounded.

"Pammy? Sammy? I don't remember." Fabio looked away, dried his eyes. "I got her a fake ID, and I got her a job here. She was running away from something."

"From what?"

"An ex-boyfriend, she said. The stalker type."

"I think the guy found her. Do you know anything about him?"

"No."

"Where is she from?"

"She wasn't specific. Back East, she said…. You sound like a detective."

"I sell bugs," said Patton proudly.

Fabio nodded as if that was slang for something terrible.

"I think her parents or someone she loved should know, don't you think?" said Patton.

"What's your name?"

"So you knew about her asthma?"

"Hell, yeah. This place was tough on her. I suggested she go back to school to be a chef like she really wanted to be."

"That's what she was doing."

Sal nodded, then smiled. He'd done something good.

Patton added, "The police can't find her next of kin. You don't know any way to tell her parents or any next of kin?"

"I wish I did. Was she working anywhere?"

"Yeah, she worked as a model through a good agency."

"Have you talked to them?"

Up until that moment, Patton had been feeling good about all he'd found so far, but such an obvious avenue had eluded him. "A good idea," he said. "Except I have a few other problems now."

"Can you give me a call if you hear anything more about Chatterley?" The man handed Patton his card.

Patton walked to his van, shaking his head. Chatterley, the police, a dead manager, a new lawyer—and where was Tess? It'd been a hell of a day. He hated to think about tomorrow.

Nearly every stoplight on the way back to the hotel was red.

CHAPTER 8 (DAY 3)

Patton hadn't slept well, his forehead throbbing and sore, his eyes too big for their sockets. Headaches were rare for him, and he usually fell asleep within minutes, to the envy of Tess. First thing he did in the morning was get $300 cash from an ATM. He tried calling Tess right away, but there was no answer. Her phone had to be off. He'd call around to hotels during lulls in his day.

The convention floor, buzzing with energy as the doors opened for the last day, swarmed with people as thick as the bugs in one of Patton's domes. On the floor with his crew, Patton made more preparations. He arranged the live bugs in their domes, but stopped that to refresh one of the brochure stands. He stopped that to straighten one of their signs. There was so much to still do. At five that day, it'd all come down. The convention center would be a madhouse as all exhibitors tore down their booths, moved stuff to their trucks, and cleaned their areas. The smaller exhibitors had only a few boxes to fill and a sign to take down, but Ben-Bugs had a lot of products and displays to pack away. They'd be there late, shipping some of the stuff by an independent trucker. The rest would go in Patton's van.

"You okay?" asked Arvid, who was finishing the domes. "You're all over the place."

"I'm telling myself I shouldn't worry. Today will be fine."

"Worry about what?"

The dead manager for one, he thought but said, "So much to do to-day."

"Have you eaten?"

"No."

"Go grab something and relax for a bit. The doors only just opened, so it'll be quiet for a while."

"You're right," said Patton.

Patton was eating a breakfast burrito in a garden lawn chair near the food area when Ronald hurried by. "Ronald," Patton called. "Where are you headed?"

"There you are. I have a guy from Sonoma interested in a large order of trichogramma. I thought you should close it. He said he'd come back in fifteen minutes." Trichogramma wasps were among the smallest of insects and were parasitic, harmless to people and animals. They had a wingspan of less than a fiftieth of an inch and attacked over two hundred species of eggs, being an efficient destroyer of many moths and butterflies—leaf eaters—in the larval stage. Three types were used in groves and orchards, and one type in vegetable gardens. Trichogramma were the most widely used beneficial insects in the world.

"Sure. Happy to," said Patton, standing, trying to cover his sense that these were his last days before his execution.

"What's wrong?"

"Just a tight schedule."

"The way you look—still have a headache?"

"Let's deal with the trichogramma," said Patton.

"You have fifteen minutes. Finish your breakfast. Sit."

Patton did. After Ronald left, four men in similar gray suits walked by, and then minutes later, two similar men rushed past. They weren't the casual clothes of conventioneers. Plain clothes police? Were they after him? Just eat, he told himself. It wasn't him.

Minutes later, his phone rang and the screen showed it was Ronald.

"There you are!" gasped Ronald.

"What's up?"

"The FBI are here with a search warrant. They're packing up anything that like looks like a file. They've also taken all our laptops."

"FBI?" Patton wondered how Chatterley's death could possibly be a federal thing.

"They asked for you, and I said you weren't here yet. Maybe you should stay away."

"They want to arrest me?"

"Don't know. Everyone's looking on," said Ronald. "I even see a news crew coming up. The FBI say it's a seizure."

"Seizure? Nothing we have is of national interest." Patton's mind whirled. Had Chatterley perhaps been undercover for the FBI? If so, what had she been looking for? Had a counter agent killed her to look like asthma? "Are they really the FBI?" he asked.

"They showed me an official document. It said something about money laundering. Apparently you accepted drug money. Is that true?"

"I didn't accept—" Then it struck him: the new financing that Tess had secured. "I told you about Tess getting venture capital. Maybe…but she couldn't—"

"Did she take drug money from a cartel in Mexico?"

"I have no idea. Tess wouldn't knowingly take dirty money," Patton said, speaking his thoughts aloud. "She's not that kind of person." Then again, he wasn't the kind of person who found dead managers.

"Have you checked out of the hotel?" Ronald said.

"No, not yet. Listen, I'll call Tess and our lawyer about all this."

"Yeah, good idea. So you want me to sign for this stuff?"

"This is some huge mistake. Let me get a hold of Tess."

"I overheard an FBI guy say they came in today because Tess had also withdrawn a lot of money this morning."

"Where's Tess now?" Patton asked.

"You don't know?"

"No."

"Tell me honestly," Ronald said. "This company isn't a front for anything, is it? You're not Walter White in Breaking Bad?"

"Of course not. Let me call you back in about a half hour, okay?"

"That's fine."

— ❦ —

Patton stuffed everything in his hotel room haphazardly into his two suitcases. Two days ago, he and Tess were royalty, set for life, and now two people had died, Tess was angry and gone, and the FBI were after them. Did he have an enemy as the lawyer had asked? Or was this all about shady financing? He felt so dizzy, he had to sit. He knew, though, he had to get out of there. The FBI maybe didn't know about the room change yesterday. If not, they'd find the mistake very soon.

Patton left the hotel from the back way. He walked straight to his van, only stopping to pick up a Las Vegas Review-Journal in front of someone's hotel room.

Although it was just after nine in the morning, the sun felt particularly hot. He guessed the temperature was already nearing a hundred.

He started his van and looked in his two side mirrors. No one seemed to be watching. As he pulled out of the lot, he kept glancing in his mirrors to see if anyone was following. No one was.

He tried Tess's phone again, but once more all he received was her voice mail.

"Tess, it's me," said Patton. "The FBI is at our booth seizing things. What's going on?" He paused, wondering if he should accuse her of something. "Just call me." After he hung up, he thought if the FBI were really after him, they'd find his position triangulating his cell phone signal, the way they'd done with O.J. Simpson. Patton had also read in PC World how much easier it was to track any cell phone now. Your cell phone had to be completely powered off for the phone to be untrackable. Maybe Tess had heard the same thing. He shouldn't use his cell phone. He powered it off. The moment felt as if he were diving into the deep end of a pool, and perhaps he couldn't swim.

He pulled into a parking lot off of Paradise Road, and he opened the newspaper. There on the top of page three was a small article about Chatterley.

Model Found Dead in Hotel

On Wednesday, police were called around 8:30 a.m. to the Edison Suites Hotel on Paradise Road after hotel security reported a guest had died from unknown causes in one of the rooms. Police confirmed that a 27-year-old woman, working as a model at the National Hardware Show at the Convention Center nearby, was found dead. Drugs are not suspected.

Autopsy reports from the Clark County coroner's office will help determine the cause. The name of the deceased woman was withheld by the coroner on Wednesday, pending notification of relatives.

Police are investigating the death, said Leonard Steele, supervisor of the Metropolitan Police Department's homicide unit, because of suspicious circumstances.

He ripped out the article as neatly as he could and stuffed it in his wallet.

As he drove down Paradise Road, heading toward the Stratosphere for no particular reason, he realized he needed to make a few decisions right this instant. Hide out or go to the convention and turn himself in? After all, his lawyer told him to hang around, but Brian hadn't known about the FBI. He'd better call Brian back—but without a cell phone, he needed to use a pay phone, which took much longer to trace. Did pay phones still exist? He could imagine Brian telling him he'd need to bring a larger retainer. With the FBI perhaps seizing their bank accounts, he might not have any money for Brian now. Did he have enough credit on his cards? Yes, but the interest rate was high.

He called Brian from a pay phone at a car wash. His secretary answered. "Is Brian in?" Patton asked.

"He's not. Would you like his voicemail?"

"Yes, please." He left a message saying the FBI was now involved perhaps because of a venture capitalist that funded his business. "You must think I'm some kind of criminal," said Patton, "but I feel like one of those jets that crash. It's always two or more things happening at once that bring it down. This financing thing has nothing to do with Chatterley, I don't think. I've turned my cell phone off, so I can't be tracked, but I'll call you later."

He clenched his hands into fists and hammered his steering wheel hard. He needed Tess now. Where would the cab have taken her? She'd made a big deal about the Bellagio and buying the tickets to Cirque du Soleil's O, even if she couldn't attend. She couldn't register under a fake name if she used her credit card, but she'd go where he wouldn't think of looking.

He took off for the Bellagio. Once there, he ran in, a man on a mission. The casino section stood in front of him, swarming with people at lunch hour, but to the left was the check-in. At the end of a long counter were the house phones. He hurried over, picked one up, and followed the directions to press O for operator.

"Operator," said an older woman.

"Tess Burch's room please."

There was a long pause, then, "She's checked out."

"Oh, no. I was to meet her. Do you know how long ago?"

"I do not, sir."

He hung up, but he was pleased he'd reasoned things out. He'd followed her thinking. Too bad he hadn't done that earlier.

He decided to check into another hotel, too, but not a big or obvious one. He drove down Las Vegas Boulevard hidden in the density of traffic, past the Stratosphere, made some turns, and noticed a small motel with the wonderful name of "Lucky Cloud." Because he was in an unlucky cloud, maybe this place would help. The paint looked fresh on the outside—completely white.

After he checked in using cash and a false name—the man didn't ask for ID—Patton called Ronald back using the pay phone near the office door. "How's it going?"

"Man," said Ronald enthusiastically. "Business is booming after the raid. Everyone wants to know what was going on. It's not like we're taking orders, but a lot of brochures are going out, and we're chatting a lot. This even beats Chatterley as a draw."

"Maybe next year I'll put the FBI in ladybug costumes."

Ronald laughed.

"So you're okay?" asked Patton.

"I'm beat, man. You coming back?"

"I'm still sorting things. Listen, I'll give you guys all an extra bonus on the next paycheck if you don't mind breaking the booth down by yourselves tonight. I'm afraid to come back. I'll call you tonight or tomorrow, okay?"

"Yeah," said Ronald.

"Thank Charlene and Arvid for me, too."

"Will do."

Afterwards, Patton held his throbbing head. He settled on the bed, feeling dizzy. It was as if he were in a whirlpool, and he was shoved toward the center, the vortex, where he'd be sliding down soon to drown. All he wanted to do was close his eyes.

CHAPTER 9 (DAY 4)

Patton awoke at daybreak, still in his clothes. After a shower, he walked to the Stratosphere where he had breakfast in a faux diner on the first floor. When he returned to his motel, he called his lawyer's office, hoping Brian was in early. He was.

"Where have you been?" Brian asked. "I've been trying to call you since last night."

Patton explained the newest wrinkle: the FBI, the money laundering investigation, and why he wasn't using his cell phone.

"How someone so nice can get into trouble so fast makes my head swirl," said Brian.

"Thanks. So what were you calling me about?"

"I managed to talk with Detective Franken again this morning. In Vegas, they work a four/ten shift schedule—four days and ten hours—so I knew I could get her early."

"And?"

"She told me about your FBI problem, so it's not news to me. Because of your new problem, she's looked at you more."

"She should look at who was after Chatterley. It wasn't me."

"I have a connection in the Vegas coroner's office, believe it or not—a college acquaintance. He says they're doing a rush on Chatterley, and the preliminary reports look like a high incidence of ragweed pollen in Chatterley's nose, throat and inhaler."

"Ragweed? Does Las Vegas even have ragweed?"

"Don't know. Point is, ragweed doesn't go in inhalers. Someone caused her to purposely have an allergic reaction—a reaction that killed her. And your fingerprints are on the inhaler."

He had to catch his breath. "It's not me."

73   CHAPTER 9

"There's too much circumstantial evidence."

"I certainly did not have ragweed. And ragweed, best I remember, flourishes in late summer and fall. Where would someone get ragweed this time of year?"

"She thinks because you're in the lawn and garden business, you probably have access to ragweed whenever you want it. She wants you to turn yourself in."

"How do we get them to look elsewhere?"

"We don't. What's clear is she and the D.A. are building a case against you for murder."

Patton stared into the white cinderblock wall. "Did you explain how the book was evidence?"

"What book? Lady Chatterley's Lover?"

"Yes, the one that's now gone."

"The one from the car with your fingerprints all over it?"

"Are you saying I should've wiped off my fingerprints? Hey, someone gave the book to her manager, who gave it to her."

"Yes, and he's now dead at a time while you were there."

"You don't believe me!"

"I'm trying to point out how justice is not necessarily about getting things right. It's about what can be proved. Let's meet soon so we can come up with a plan—such as getting my private detective to work on following up some of your leads. I need to also go over the timeline and specifics more carefully with you. And get a retainer."

"So I'm not turning myself in?"

"Not right away."

"Money? How much?"

"I was going to say ten thousand up front, but now with the FBI thing, I have a hell of a lot to do for you."

Patton said nothing. With the FBI likely freezing his bank account, money was going to be a huge issue. Maybe his mother could lend him some money. Maybe Brian knew that and purposely didn't mention Mom.

"Can you fly back today?" Brian said.

"I drove. "

"That's four or five hours. Hop in your car now."

"I was planning to, but maybe I should look at a few things."

"Such as what? If you stay there, they could arrest you, probably within the day if the D.A. has his way. He's an asshole, from what I've learned. He'll put an affidavit together and get a warrant for your arrest."

"If I leave, won't I be fleeing or something? Or are you saying if I'm in L.A., I won't be arrested?"

"It'll be delayed. We'll work out a deal where, instead of extradition, you'll return and give yourself up."

"Explain to me why I'm even a suspect," Patton said. "If I'd killed her, wouldn't I have fled or moved her body or something?"

"As I understood through Franken—if I grasp her thinking right—this was your plan."

"I'm not following."

"She thinks you were feeling guilty about your affair, so when you learned the girl had this asthma problem, you had an instant solution. If you could put something in her inhaler, she would have what looked like an accidental death, and you'd be free."

"Why would I want a dead person in my hotel room? My name would be in the paper and my wife would find out—as she did two nights ago and left me—so Chatterley's death is, believe me, no help."

"I pointed that out, too. Franken said you probably thought Chatterley would die at home, but things happened faster than you expected."

"This is so ludicrous, I can't even describe it."

"And now with the FBI after you, they're thinking they have their man."

Patton had to hold the phone against his chest for a second because he thought he'd scream or smash the phone against the wall.

"Maybe Chatterley's parents or friends know of someone who wanted her dead," Patton said.

"She hasn't been ID'd yet. Fingerprints and dental records have brought nothing so far."

"Isn't that odd? Doesn't this seem suspicious even to the police?"

"Not really," said Brian. "They're mainly concerned with who killed her, and they think it's you."

"Why would they want to ruin my life? They'll spend, what, months prosecuting me while, right now, the crime is getting cold. Clues are surely being lost."

"My detective will find them."

"Why am I paying for something the police should be doing?"

"It's just the system."

"I'll drive back to L.A. this morning."

"I just remembered, I have to be in court this afternoon," said Brian. "You'll have to speak with my assistant. She's very capable."

"Assistant? I'm dyin' here. I can't—"

CHAPTER 9

"Or first thing tomorrow morning, how's that? Drive back now. We'll meet Saturday morning, nine a.m. at my office. Just get out of Las Vegas, though, as soon as you can."

Patton next spoke to Ronald, who was in his car driving back to Los Angeles and said the dismantling of the booth had gone well. "That police detective also came by last night," he said.

"Franken?"

"That's her."

Arvid and Charlene's voices broke into the background, but Patton couldn't make out their words. "I didn't kill Chatterley," he said to pre-empt them.

"I told her you're a good guy, a good employer," said Ronald. "I also said I thought this Chatterley had asthma. Wasn't that what it was?"

"Yes, but Chatterley had been afraid of something. I think her former lover was stalking her. Now Franken is suspecting me."

"I told her you're not a murderer."

"I'm not."

"She wanted to know where you were. Of course, I didn't know. So what's going on? Are we going to have jobs?"

"Yes, your jobs are fine, and I can't explain what the hell's going on," said Patton. "I don't know if the FBI's raid of our booth and Chatterley's murder are connected. I can't find Tess."

"You haven't reached Tess yet?" said Ronald.

Patton sighed. How much should Ronald know? "I have to be truthful, guy. Tess and I were going through some hard times that came to a head just before this."

"But you two are the best couple in the world," Ronald blurted. "You have such a wonderful give-and-take. If you two have problems, what kind of hope does someone like me have?"

Again, Arvid and Charlene instantly commented, but he couldn't tell what.

"It's not in my job description to be a marital role model," Patton said.

"You don't think she's hurt, too, do you?"

"Why would you say that?"

"The FBI guys mentioned the guy you took money from is danger-ous. 'Does your boss know who he's dealing with?' one said. We're kind of scared."

A darkness fell over Patton. He hoped to hell Tess was safe. "I don't think she knew, but Tess has to be okay. Don't even think otherwise."

— ❦ —

The day had warmed up. In his van, he cranked the air conditioner on high and pulled on his sunglasses, ready for two more stops. Before he tried the modeling agency, he stopped at a CVS Pharmacy and bought a calling card. At the corner was a pay phone. He called his mother, who he'd need to ask for money.

"Hello," she said warily.

"It's me, your son," said Patton.

"Sammy, nice to hear from you—why does it say 'Blocked ID?'"

"No, it's your son. I'm at a pay phone."

"I'm kind of mad at you, Sam."

"Sam? I'm not— Do you have visitors there? Perhaps the FBI?"

"Yes. Say, it's not a good time to talk because I'm hoping to hear from my son, who messed up or some fuck."

"I'm sorry, Mom. It's not what you might think."

"His wife's done something, too."

"Yeah, I'm trying to find her. Don't know where she is."

"She said some offshore bank wired her one and a half million dollars instead of just a half million, so she had to wire back one million to some place in Nevada. Crazy, eh?" His mother made it sound light-hearted, but Patton realized she was trying to explain Tess's money laundering—accidental. She must have spoken to Tess before this all came down.

"Where might I find her?" he asked.

"Got to go now. Bye."

"Don't be mad at me. I love you."

She said nothing but just hung up.

CHAPTER 10

Patton jumped into his van. He wanted to meet the agent who knew Chatterley. Tess had said Beyond Convention Model and Talent specialized in professional models for conventions and advertising. He didn't know where it was located, but using the pay phone at the motel, with help from information, he'd called. He learned the agency was downtown "near the new Clark County Regional Justice Center," which had no meaning for him, but the receptionist gave him directions to Lewis Avenue.

He arrived and walked through the wide doors. Beyond Convention's lobby featured lush white carpeting, marble wainscoting, and black-and-white blowups of gorgeous women, dream women with pillow lips and fiery eyes that suggested the essence of a sexual soul. The couch by the windows was book-ended by giant split-leaf philodendrons. He strode up to the receptionist's desk that stood guard to a set of double doors and smiled at the coffee-skinned woman who could easily be one of the models. Her nametag said "Amanda."

"Hello, Amanda," said Patton. "I'm here about a model."

"To book one for a professional shoot?"

"A convention, actually, and it's about a model who helped out at our booth. She died, I learned." He didn't need to tell her she died in his room.

"Chatterley," said Amanda. "Just a moment. You'll want to talk with the head of the agency, Joan Rivers."

"Joan Rivers? The comedian? I thought she died."

Amanda shook her head. "Someone else. Very different. Your name?"

"Patton Burch."

She spoke into her phone. "A Mr. Burch is here to see you about Chatterley…yes…okay, be right there." She hung up. "Excuse me a moment, will you?"

"By all means," he said, and Amanda opened one of the double doors and tapped in her high heels down the marble floor toward a set of glass-sided offices.

In less than two minutes, Amanda returned. "I'm sorry," she said. "Ms. Rivers said she spoke to the police already. She's sorry, but she's now very busy."

"That's kind of odd, isn't it? Particularly if I need another model."

"I can have you speak with one of our booking agents. Would you like that?"

"I want to speak to Joan Rivers."

"She's very busy. You really need an appointment for her."

"Can you get me one?"

"Not for today."

"May I just wait?"

"It won't do you any good. She's a very busy woman."

"I'll wait. Thanks," he said.

"But there's no point."

"I'm patient."

She shrugged. As he sat on the couch, he thought this was stupid. He could be there all day—they wouldn't care. As he considered his options, he noticed some thin spidery threads on the broad leaves of a philodendron near him. He scooted over and examined it more closely. He saw the receptionist watch him, and that was good. "Oh, no," he muttered. He touched a specific spot on a leaf, then looked closely at his finger.

"What?" the secretary asked.

He looked under the leaf and shook his head like a doctor finding a serious condition. "Spider mites."

"Spiders?" She frowned.

"Spider mites—very small. You can see the faint webbing here in the gap in the leaf, and if you shake a leaf over a clean piece of paper, little spiders will fall onto it. These mites can kill this beautiful plant."

"Oh, my gosh," she said, grabbing a piece of paper from her printer and stepping over quickly in her high-heeled shoes.

"Hold the paper under the leaf," he said, standing, directing, and stepping back slightly. "And shake it. Shake it hard." While she was shaking away, he moved quickly and quietly to the door that led back to the offices. As the door closed, he could hear her say, "My gosh, you're right, little spiders."

He hurried down the hallway and saw an open door. The nameplate on the glass said Joan Rivers, and he found Ms. Rivers, a blonde in her late thirties with a fondness for blue eye shadow. She looked up with a frown. He smiled.

"Did Amanda send you in?"

"Amanda's dealing with a serious spider mite issue. I'm Patton Burch. We'd hired Chatterley."

"As I've mentioned, I spoke to the police already. It's being dealt with."

"It? Chatterley happened to be your employee, a wonderful person, and you don't seem to give a shit. Why?"

"Of course I care, but if you don't leave, I'll call the police. They said you're a person of interest."

"Like I'm the murderer? Is that what they meant?"

"Yes, they asked that I avoid you." Her steely blue eyes ground into him.

"Whoever killed Chatterley is still out there. The police don't seem to care—do you?"

"The detective, in fact, asked that I contact her if I heard from you." She reached for the phone.

"Go ahead. Callous agency squishes innocent client—might make for some bad press."

"Bad press is good press."

"If you're willing to take that chance. Is the owner happy that one of your models is dead?"

She hung up the phone. "I'm the owner, and I'm not happy."

Just then, Amanda was at her door, saying, "He slipped past me. I didn't—"

"That's okay, dear," said Joan. "I'll deal with him." She offered the chair in front of her desk. "Two minutes is all you get."

"I just have a few questions," he said sitting. "As you probably know, Chatterley is an assumed name. The coroner doesn't know who she is."

"It occurred to me that the name Chatterley Langstrump wasn't her birth name, but she had a valid driver's license."

He took out a pen he had in his pocket to write notes. "Langstrump? I wonder if that's German," he said. He wrote on a receipt from his wallet.

"You never heard of Pippi Longstocking?" said Rivers. "In Norway, the name is Langstrump. Pippi Langstrump was one of my heroes when I was a kid."

"So Chatterley's name was super fake?"

"She had a driver's license that said differently."

"Do you happen to have any resume or history on her?"

"As I told the police earlier today, I had little. From the way she walked the runway, it was clear she was an experienced model. And she could pose. She understood the camera, and her personality just shined. I might have been able to sell her more knowing her background, but she just wanted part-time work at conventions. I figured once she gained my trust, I might use her more."

"You have any idea where she's from?"

"Maine, she said, but I didn't believe her."

"Why?"

"She didn't have that kind of accent."

"How about San Francisco?" he tried.

"She seemed West Coast to me, yes, and there are some great modeling agencies in San Francisco. She could have learned her walk and poses there."

"But doesn't every big city in the country have modeling agencies?"

"Only the big agencies have the resources to make a top model. That'd be in New York, Miami, Chicago, Los Angeles, and San Francisco. If we're talking West Coast, that's two cities."

"Did you tell the police this?"

"They didn't ask. They wanted to know about you. But I'd only dealt with your wife."

He nodded. If only he could deal with his wife. "Anything else you know about Chatterley?"

"Annie Leibovitz is a big photographer, and I swore one of the nearly naked women in an ad that Leibovitz shot was Chatterley. Chatterley only smiled when I suggested it."

"How do I get a hold of Annie Leibovitz?"

"You want to go to New York? I doubt you'll get to see her."

Ms. Rivers looked at her desk as if considering more. "Chatterley was a smart girl—a curious mind. We sometimes talked politics, other times, food and wine. Girls like her have a tough time in modeling, though, even if Leibovitz shot her."

"Why?"

"She knew that her beauty got her things. Jobs that play on sexual tension, such as actress, waitress, and model, seem to dig at some girls at the heart-and-soul level. They can feel like they're a fraud. I told her if she's got it, flaunt it. But the world tends to dehumanize the Chatterleys of the world."

He thought of the way the first policemen looked at Chatterley, as if she somehow deserved it. "Whoever she was running away from might have wanted to do her in. Anything you know about that?"

She paused as if a vague thought was getting clearer. "She mentioned once a couple of her instructors, who were big name chefs here in Vegas, were hitting on her. She said her program had a lot of female students, so she wasn't the only one getting attention. When I called her for your job, she was eager for it as if she needed to get away from school."

"Or perhaps a person from her past?"

She shrugged. "I'm sorry I can't help you more. I'm also sorry I didn't let you in, but you're not the police."

"No—just your client." He peered at her directly. "Chatterley didn't deserve to die." He stood and held out his hand. She shook it.

"I hope you can help find who did her in," she said.

"I do, too."

As Patton left the building for his van and the day's heat pushed at him, so did the knowledge that pieces were falling into place. Chatterley's killer might be up in San Francisco, someone who Chatterley tried to avoid purposely, someone she knew. The man seemed relentless, intimidating, and worked through stealth—someone he needed to be careful around once he found him. Maybe when he saw his lawyer in the morning, these facts might add to "reasonable doubt" if they went to trial.

He jumped onto the I-15 South and headed home. As his tires whirred on the hot concrete, he realized that from all the looks Chatterley had received at the booth, she had been a magnet all the time. There could be some geek she'd barely even noticed who had become obsessed. Still, it was someone who knew about her asthma. That should narrow things down. A boyfriend or her father seemed the two possibilities. After all, there had been the note in Chatterley's cookbook about her angry father.

As he drove through the arid treeless beige country where shrubs were like chocolate chips, he passed the outposts of casinos on the border with California, and he considered Chatterley's death from a detective's point of view. How could the pollen get into Chatterley's inhaler? He seriously doubted that anyone could break into his hotel bedroom while they both slept, rummaging in her purse and being so quiet that they didn't wake up. He bet that in this dry environment where most asthma patients avoided problems, Chatterley didn't normally need or carry around her inhaler.

She probably had it when she worked the casino, but she left that job.

Then it struck him—so simple. On most days, the inhaler had probably just been in a drawer. Yet she was carrying the inhaler that day, so something had triggered her asthma again. Assuming that her bedroom was a place she had lived in at least eight hours a day, a trigger there was likely. Brilliant: the person who broke into her room not only took something but also left something—the pollen. He'd have inserted pollen into her inhaler, and then left a little pollen around the room that would require her to use her inhaler. Pollen was an irritant, not a poison, so it wasn't something that would send her into shock immediately. That last dose from her inhaler after Patton and she had had dinner had been the tipping point. She'd awakened in the night unable to breathe well.

As he drove, his thoughts changed to Tess. Where was she right now? What was she thinking? Did she hate him completely? A brown tumbleweed like a ball of barbed wire rolled across the lanes in front of him, and he quickly braked. A sense of despair then swept through him unlike anything he'd known.

Fuck the FBI. He turned his phone on and pressed T for Tess, and Enter to dial. On the second ring, she answered: "Patton?"

"I didn't think I'd get you," he said, surprised.

"I turned my phone on to see if I had any voicemail. Maybe you'd left a message apologizing or saying something to make this all better."

"Apologize? What's the FBI after us for? You're the engineer of that."

"Maybe I should hang up now."

"No—please don't. I'm just trying to understand things. Where are you? Home?"

"Not home. I'm not telling you where I am."

"So this phone call is a coincidence?" said Patton. "Magic or something?"

"I'd hardly call it magic, unless having sex with a model is magic."

"I didn't sleep with her. You have to believe me."

"And you'll believe I didn't go after dirty money?"

"I would hope you didn't."

"I didn't, but I'd feel naïve if I believed you and the model."

"So be naïve."

"I can't."

"What I will apologize for is feeling our marriage slip, and I didn't talk to you about it. You've been my partner, my best friend, and yet I found it hard to talk about what I was feeling." When she didn't say anything, he said, "So, the FBI thing—I don't understand how you got us here."

"None of it makes sense to me, either," said Tess.

"Tell me a few things. Mom briefly explained our investor—Birnam?—sent you a million dollars by mistake?"

"He said his bank in the Cayman Islands made the error of adding in the million, and the easiest way to fix it was for me to wire him back to his Nevada bank."

"And you wired it back to him?"

"Why not? It wasn't our money."

"It's called laundering. I'm wondering if he did this before with someone else."

"Why?"

"Maybe he finds someone like you every time he needs some more cash cleaned."

"How do you know this stuff?"

"He was clearly playing into your need and hopes."

"Our needs and hopes."

"Yes, ours."

She didn't say anything for a moment, and he thought he should stay quiet, too.

"Have you spoken to your mother about this?" she said.

"I tried. The FBI was there."

"I'm not sure we can get back together," Tess said, "especially if you're going to be in jail for a while."

"And you're not going to be in jail?"

"How'd we get into these messes?"

"Let me give you Brian Feinberg's number. He's my lawyer, and he can help you, too. He's also a good person to give a message to for me." He gave her Brian's number.

"I don't think we should be on our cell phones anymore," she said.

"I suppose." So this was it.

"Patton?"

"Yeah?"

"Thanks for the call." And then she hung up.

— ✿ —

Patton arrived back at their Eagle Rock home just after sunset. He'd figured in this post-9/11 world, the FBI didn't have the resources to stake out a house for days, particularly if they'd searched it already. He, Patton, wasn't their prime suspect anyway, and by now they may be finding that

Tess wasn't intentionally involved in money laundering. He wasn't worried about sleeping here. He'd keep the lights off.

The view from the hilltop showed the lights of Greater Los Angeles pooled into sections, divided by the dark hills. To the left, the skyscrapers of downtown stood like huddled chess pieces with red lights at their crowns, blinking. Further to the right was Hollywood, and the lighted swath, Hollywood Boulevard. The dome of the Griffith Park Observatory nestled above, like an eye, unblinking. Even further to the right was the bulk of Griffith Park, dark in the night, where the homeless sought shelter and teenagers prayed for privacy.

With his troubles, he might not keep this house or this panoramic view much longer. Nothing was permanent. Chatterley knew.

CHAPTER II (DAY 5)

Patton awoke to a hammering sound and the doorbell ringing again and again. He lurched up in bed, heart pounding, and looked at the clock. Six-thirty a.m. The FBI, he realized from the morning news shows, liked early-morning rousts. He'd been wrong about the FBI. He shouldn't have slept here. The FBI's perps were always handcuffed and paraded before the news cameras. Was he about to be on the morning news in his underwear? He quickly grabbed his black silk robe from the closet and hurried downstairs. "I'm coming," he shouted.

Patton took a deep breath and opened the door, ready for the perp walk. His mother stood before him, scowling.

"Mom, thank God."

"You're happy?" she said, walking in, her short blond hair combed perfectly as if she just came from the hairdresser.

"What's going on? Why so early?" he said.

She was dressed in black slacks and a stylish white top with a string of pearls. This was her casual wear. "So what the hell were you thinking?" she demanded. He shut the door after her and felt as he did at ten year's old when his baseball had gone through a neighbor's window.

"About the FBI? That wasn't my doing."

"You have another woman here?"

"For crying out loud, Mom. You think I'm some player?"

"I don't know what to think."

"Since when did you become so chummy with Tess and take her side?"

"She's my daughter-in-law. Of course I listen."

"That's new."

"I adore her."

"She's never felt that. She always feels under your magnifying glass."

"There's a lot to see."

He laughed. "You want some biscotti?"

"How about coffee?"

"I haven't made it yet."

"I'll take what I can get."

They walked into the kitchen. Patton reached into one of the glass-fronted cupboards and pulled out two small dessert plates, which he placed on the dark granite countertop. From another cupboard, he pulled down a tin can and pulled out two plain biscotti, placing them on the plates. He gave one plate to his mother, who was sitting at the round, Danish-modern breakfast table.

"Thanks," she said. "Tess explained to me how she'd been fooled into laundering money and also that you're the prime suspect in this girl's murder."

"Which is because of this FBI thing. I was in the wrong place at the right time a few times." He left out the part about the dead manager.

"Don't they need evidence with the girl?"

"A detective seems to think it's a slam-dunk case. The young woman died from pollen ingestion, and I, of course, being in the home-and-garden field, gave her the pollen."

"Did you?"

He glared at her. His own mother? "Of course not. Why would I want to kill someone?"

"Desperate people do desperate things."

"I wasn't desperate, Mom."

"So you've called Brian?"

"Yes, I'm meeting him in—" He glanced to the Bavarian clock they had on the wall. "In about two hours." From another cupboard, he pulled out a can of Trader Joe's coffee.

"It sounded from Tess that you don't have a lot of money right now. I can help you. I don't have a lot of liquid cash, but I can sell something."

"You're on a fixed income—don't be silly." Then again, he was supposed to bring a check for Brian's retainer.

"It's worth it," she said.

"Actually, if you can spot me ten thousand for the retainer, I'll pay you back."

"Ten thousand?"

"I'm sorry, Mom."

She nodded, pulling out her checkbook from her purse. "Did you and Tess not have enough drama in your life, and this spices things up? I always said you should have had some children. They make you crazy in another way, but at least you're not in the papers. It's not too late for kids."

"It is if your wife doesn't want to sleep with you." He scooped four tablespoons of coffee into his Krups coffee maker and filled the water tank to the right level.

"My mother-in-law, your grandmother, once gave me advice about marriage after my honeymoon, and it was 'Remember to spend as much time on the bottom as you do on the top.'"

He winced. "Sex advice now, Mom?"

She laughed. "I thought she was talking sex, too, which I'd newly discovered. Years later, I realized she was talking about not always being right. Admit when you're on the bottom."

"Believe me, I'm on the bottom."

"Leave early, dear. You know how the traffic is to Century City."

"It's a Saturday."

"I just worry. Here I am seventy years old, and I still worry about my child."

"Don't worry," he said.

Nonetheless, later, as he drove to Brian's office, he worried. He always thought of Tess as his twin. They thought similarly, they fought similarly. They completed each other. The writer Kurt Vonnegut had invented a word for what they had—a duprass. They lived lives around each other, and nothing could invade that. It was them against the world. Now the emptiness he felt could fill a hundred swimming pools.

Patton pulled off Interstate 10 and worked his way through the expensive neighborhood of Cheviot Hills. Century City was in an odd spot. Once a back lot for 20th-Century Fox, Century City rose in the sixties in the midst of a residential neighborhood to become what was then the city of the future—wide boulevards, gleaming skyscrapers, and no telephone poles or visible parking lots. The Beverly Hills freeway was supposed to shuttle people there, but Beverly Hills didn't want a freeway to bisect its city, so it was never built. Let poorer areas be split by a freeway.

As he drove down the Avenue of the Americas, Century City felt faceless and sterile, but it was an important business center with many executives and law firms. A parking ramp took him a few stories underground. Because it was a Saturday, there were plenty of open spaces in the visitors area.

The elevator brought Patton to the double-wide doors of the law offices of Fallon, Tour, and Feinberg, and Brian stood there holding open the door and smiling as if they were going to drink mint juleps at the race track. Brian was dressed in a crisp white shirt, a pressed beige suit, and a red tie—odd for a Saturday. Brian was much shorter than Patton, perhaps five feet five, and he had the kind of tan one received from golf greens.

"You dress this way on a Saturday?" said Patton. He held out his hand and they shook.

"Didn't I tell you that you needed to wear a suit today and bring another?" said Brian. Patton himself dressed most days as he did now: khaki pants and a knit shirt.

"A suit?"

"We have to fly to Las Vegas, where you'll be booked and processed. You'll want to be in a suit before the police today and a judge on Monday."

Patton gasped. "I thought you said it'd be a few days—to plan."

"That was yesterday, and they acted faster than I expected. It's official. Ms. Langstrump's death is a homicide. Anaphylactic shock induced by pollen. I made arrangements for us to go later this afternoon."

"I can't. I have things to do. This is too quick."

"No, no. It's arranged. I'll go with you to Vegas and help you. Come," said Brian. "Let's go to my office."

As they walked down the hall past office after office—this was a major law firm—Brian said, "You barely look older than the last time I saw you at your mother's house."

"That must have been five years ago."

"Yeah."

As they strode into his spacious corner office, Patton could see hiring Brian was going to cost him a lot. One of the walls' several paintings was in a style that looked familiar. He moved closer. It showed a young man swimming underwater in a pool.

"An original Hockney," Brian said proudly.

Patton nodded. "I brought a check from my mother for your retainer."

"Excellent. Have a seat."

"I'm not ready to go to Las Vegas today, though."

"We have to. I have a time crunch, and I may not be able to help you if you let them extradite you, which means the LAPD will come arrest you, handcuff you, and you'll be driven to Las Vegas in the back of a squad car. It's much easier for us to fly in and surrender under our own terms."

Patton sat in the leather Barcelona chair in front of Brian's massive cherry wood desk. "Will it at least go fast?"

"Nothing's guaranteed, mind you, but the way it usually works is once we check in at the precinct station, Detective Franken will escort us to a room where you'll be questioned some more. Then you'll be taken to the jail where you'll be booked, photographed, and fingerprinted."

"A mug shot like O.J.?"

"There is no good mug shot."

"So how long does all this take?"

"That part might only take a half hour. However, until we can see a judge for arraignment—on Monday morning—you have to be in jail."

"What?" Now this was too much. "I just want to make bail."

"You have to see a judge first."

"But there goes two more days when I can be investigating."

"It's private detective time. That'll add to expenses. And do you have money for bail?"

Patton was still processing being in jail. He couldn't be in jail. And the cost. "Will bail be reasonable, say under a hundred thousand?"

"Unlikely. It's Capital Two murder with malice aforethought. It's up to the judge—no guarantees—lucky to get bail at all. But turning yourself in like this will help."

"Can I put up my house for bail?"

"We'll need a current appraisal, tax records showing the current tax liabilities, and a mortgage statement from the lender—all easy to do. Let's hope your house can cover it. Is your wife listed on the deed?"

Patton nodded.

"Will she sign for you?"

"I don't even know where she is."

"Well," Brian said, reaching for a square of paper on his desk. "She called and left you a message." Brian held out the paper, and Patton looked at it. It said, Tess called and said she can't tell you where she is, but call her, and it gave a phone number. Patton did not keep a list of Tess's girlfriends' phone numbers, but he recognized this one because it ended in 1234. Her friend Cindy had once bragged to him how she made the phone company give her a good phone number when she moved after her divorce.

"Did Tess talk with you?" Patton asked.

"No. She just left the message. Can you count on her co-signing the deed?"

"I can't say that."

"This will be a problem then."

"What are we talking about for bail?"

"A million or more—maybe the equity in your house isn't enough, unless you go with a bail bondsman."

"Is this a joke?"

"The charge is murder. Some murder cases have no bail. I hope to get it reduced, of course, but either you fork over cash or property or pay ten percent to a bail bondsman—or maybe your mother will put up her house?"

"Maybe."

"We can call her on our way. We need to stop at the Men's Wearhouse and get you a suit."

"Why can't I go home and get one?"

Brian looked at his watch, then snapped his fingers. "You live near your mother, right?"

"Yes, near Eagle Rock."

"The Burbank airport is close to there. I'll change our reservations to Burbank airport. We can get your suit and stop to see your mother to get and sign a few papers. Call her on the way. Yes, this could work out." He looked like a boy who had filled in the last blank on a final test.

"You don't need to hold my hand," Patton said. "I'll stop off, grab my suit, and meet you at my mother's. Okay?"

"Sounds like a plan."

Patton, however, had a different plan.

— ❦ —

After leaving Brian's office, Patton made a beeline to Cindy Hartwick's house, a Spanish colonial in Beverlywood, an area nearby and always referred to in the real estate section as "Beverly Hills Adjacent." Patton and Tess had once lived in the area, and their elderly neighbor had told them that Beverlywood and Cheviot Hills had been bean fields and orange groves in the thirties. Now there were only large and elegant homes. Cindy wasn't Tess's best friend, but they were friendly. Cindy had not worked when she was married. Childless, Cindy was forever improving herself, going to a law-school prep course one time, a real estate course another.

He'd only been to Cindy's once, when Tess's car wouldn't start there, and Patton had come to rescue her. He had a vague memory of where it was, and he slowly cruised the street that he was sure it was on. Cindy stood out because, at that time, she was recently divorced and angry about it. "Don't trust men," she'd told Tess, but Patton knew that Cindy was the one who'd had the affair. Cindy had explained to Tess that her husband had essentially pushed her away, always saying that he wasn't good enough for her, that depression ran in his family. He'd never particularly liked Cindy. She was the kind of woman who'd purposely drive over roadkill.

He spotted the house. He recognized the plum and magnolia trees that had become so overgrown and unruly that the resulting shade made her lawn mostly bare dirt. Chaotic strands of red bougainvillea swallowed a wall. The plastic trashcans by her front stairs offered the effect of an extended middle finger to her neighbors whose yards had lawns one could sink into. With white paint starting to peel from the stucco, Cindy's home had a sense of abandonment, which paralleled how Cindy had felt.

Tess's Lexus was parked on the street. Patton parked his van a block up. He rang Cindy's doorbell. The door opened, and Cindy, with long wet red hair, stood before him in a white robe, looking defiant, more like a teenager than a woman in her mid-thirties.

"Ah, the slime bucket," she said.

"Nice to see you, too, Cindy. Let me talk to Tess."

"She's not here."

"Her car?" He pointed across the street.

"She borrowed mine to get some eggs, but she doesn't want to see you."

"She needs me—we need each other—"

"Right," she said. "Romeo and Juliet you're not."

"—To get out of this mess."

"Just leave."

"Tess," he yelled. "Tess!"

"Get out of here," said Cindy, now pushing him. He pushed back— then pressed hard and past her into the living room, whose massive leather sectional was for a much larger room. "Tess," he shouted again.

Tess ran in, wearing black jeans and a silk blouse, and her hair was newly cut and layered as if she were trying on a new persona. She frowned. He apparently was a problem she did not want to tackle now.

Cindy yelled, "I'm calling the police if you don't get out right now."

"That might bring the FBI on your girlfriend," said Patton. "You want that?"

Cindy dashed across the room and reached under the couch, pulling out a shotgun. It didn't look fancy or particularly big—just two barrels and a trigger. "Then how about this, Mr. Bigman? Out!"

"Cindy," said Tess. "We don't need this. If anyone shoots Patton, it'll be me, so put the gun down."

Cindy shook her head. "Why?"

"Because maybe we need cooler heads right now. Let me talk with my husband."

"Don't fool yourself."

Tess looked hard at Patton. "Maybe you should leave, after all."

"Just give me a couple minutes. I've got some ideas."

Tess stared at him skeptically, but then nodded. Cindy lowered her weapon, returned to the couch, and shoved the gun underneath. "It's a mistake," said Cindy.

"How did you find me here?" said Tess to Patton.

"Doesn't matter. We need to put our heads together on this Birnam thing. What if we could help the FBI? They're not going to go away, you know."

"It's my problem. I'm using our company lawyer, Bob Trenton."

"This kind of situation is beyond his expertise. Use Brian Feinberg," said Patton, his hands out.

"I'll leave you two lovebirds alone then," said Cindy with a smirk, moving past Patton and Tess toward a hallway and the back of the house. They both watched her go. Cindy's sad life was what their lives could be if they didn't repair their problems.

"How did you end up talking to Birnam in the first place?" Patton asked.

"I mean really—you're here to help me? Don't you have bigger problems with your murder charge?"

"I found you, didn't I, so maybe I can help you, too? How'd you connect with Birnam?"

"Every venture capitalist I went to, if they said no or had terms I didn't like, I asked if they had any recommendations for someone else. One guy gave me Birnam's name and number. Birnam seemed on the up-and-up."

"Did he have an office, a secretary?"

"Probably. He gave me his cell phone number, so I always reached him directly."

"Did you call the guy who recommended him?"

"Yes. It turns out he doesn't know Birnam beyond meeting him at a Beverly Hills party. He's convinced Birnam is for real, though."

"If Birnam has that much money and the FBI is watching, maybe he's in the mob. Maybe your life is in danger, here."

"He didn't seem dangerous to me. He was friendly, perhaps a bit of a name dropper—Elton John, Celine Dion, Siegfried and Roy."

Chapter 11

"All Vegas shows. Did he spend a lot of time in Las Vegas?"

"I don't know. I didn't do anything wrong except think this was the best for us. I always thought about us."

"I thought about us, too."

"Not with that woman," she said. "You know, fuck it. We're not getting anywhere."

He took a deep breath. "We love each other and have a good marriage, and you know that."

"What do you really want, Patton?"

"Do you want me to go to jail for murder?"

She stared at him. "I'm mad."

"I know. And I'm sorry. But if you don't want me to spend a lot of time in jail, we need to put up our house up for bail. Will you co-sign?"

She stared at him. "I don't want to, no."

"What?" He said it perhaps a little too loudly because she stepped backed and blinked, but he hadn't moved toward her.

"I don't know. Maybe. This is too much for me."

"And me? I didn't kill her. I'm supposed to spend years of my life for something I didn't do? The police aren't investigating. I'm the only one asking around who our model was because someone did kill her. All I know is that she likely worked as a model through a good agency in this city or San Francisco—or perhaps New York or Miami. She had asthma. She may have worked as a cocktail waitress serving white nuns—the drink, not the holy women."

"At Tosca, you mean?"

"Tosca?"

"Tosca Café in North Beach. On our trip to San Francisco, don't you remember the food tour we took?"

"What?"

"Tosca was a fifties kind of place, had a jukebox with Sinatra and Italian arias on it."

"Oh, yeah."

"And their specialty drink's called a white nun—brandy, Kahlua and steamed milk. It's what they're known for. You think she worked there?"

He couldn't stop smiling. "How do you remember this stuff?"

"I like Kahlua…. Are you doing what I think?"

"You don't need any specifics. I just know I can do more for myself by not being in jail. I studied as a scientist. I can find things. Can I call you here?"

"No. If you found me here, so will the FBI."

"We'll use my lawyer Brian as an intermediary, okay? Please call him tomorrow. And if I can help you with Birnam, I will."

"How?"

"We need to find him."

"If I knew how, don't you think I'd do it? His cell phone number no longer works. I have no address beyond what turns out to be a private post box masking as a suite number, and the box is now closed. He scammed me."

"We have to work together," he said.

She stared at him hard—but she nodded, and a surge went through him. He had hope. "Okay, then," he said and stepped to the door.

She followed. As he opened the door, she leaned in and kissed him quickly on the cheek. He turned and kissed her full on the lips, and she returned it with passion.

"All right," he said, smiling, and left.

He drove immediately to their house. There, he printed several four-by-six copies of the photo of Chatterley he'd taken with his phone. Photoshop allowed him to sharpen the photo and give it better contrast. He also packed for a week and included his suit. You never know when you have to look presentable. Feeling paranoid, he pulled his van into the garage, worrying that there might be an APB on his vehicle or whatever the Las Vegas police or FBI might do. He pulled the magnetic BenBugs car magnet signs off of either side, and he grabbed a small brush and fast-drying white paint and sat before his license plate, which read BENBUGS. He painted out letters on either side so it read ENBU. People might think it was his last name. He blew on the letters to help dry it, and as he looked at his work critically, he could see the first and last letters were still raised. He opened the garage door and stepped to one of his flowerbeds, which were automatically watered each morning. Scooping up some of the wet clay-like dirt on the edges, he dabbled it artfully on the license plate, especially on the white raised letters to make the plate look dirty. It was better, but the whole clean backside looked out of place for a dirty license plate, so he flung handfuls of mud at the rear.

He loaded the van, locked the house, and drove to the bank, where he found his business accounts were indeed frozen. His savings account, however, which didn't have a lot of money in it, still worked. He withdrew a couple thousand in cash. He didn't want to leave a paper trail using credit cards.

He did not call his mother or Brian, who must be together and worrying. He'd leave a message for them later. Time was of the essence.

CHAPTER 12

A little after one, Patton made it to Coalinga, halfway to San Francisco. He pulled into the Harris Ranch where he called his mother from a pay phone. She and Brian probably would be pissed—and maybe even Brian would abandon Patton.

Patton only received her answering machine. "Hey, Mom. It's Patton. I'm sorry I didn't show up, but I have good reason. Apologies to Brian, too. I'll explain later today or tomorrow from a pay phone. Love you."

At nearly five p.m., Patton crossed the Bay Bridge and headed toward the only hotel he knew, the Pacific Regent on Fisherman's Wharf. Tess had booked it for them on their getaway winter weekend a few years earlier, the one where they went to the Tosca Café. While it had rained most of the time, they had a great time eating, drinking, and taking a bus tour to the wine country. That was one of the best things about Tess—she really relaxed and had fun when she traveled. Soon, he hoped to hunker down and research using his laptop and the hotel's wifi.

As Patton drove on the edge of the wharf, sailboats and the Golden Gate Bridge stood in the distance. He came to the hotel and swung around the fountain into the valet parking lane. He grimaced at the posted daily parking rate. Welcome to San Francisco. When a valet opened his door, Patton said, "Don't park it yet. I don't have a reservation, so I want to make sure I can get a room."

"No problem," said the man.

The marble-tiled registration area could be right out of 2001: A Space Odyssey—modern and white. One counter had two computer screens for self-check-in. Another counter had three registration clerks. Patton strode up to a young man with short-cropped hair and asked for a room.

"For how many nights?" said the clerk.

"At least two, maybe more."

The man tapped away. "Yes, we do. Your name?"

"Johnson," said Patton.

The man typed it in. "First name?"

"Mr."

"Mr?" The man raised his eyebrows.

"Olaf. Mr. Olaf Johnson," said Patton.

"And I need a credit card, Mr. Johnson," said the man.

"I have a credit card problem. May I pay with cash?"

"Yes. You'll need to pay upfront and leave fifty-dollars-a-night deposit, too."

The man gave him the rate, which seemed steep. Patton didn't want to spend such a large chunk of his savings here.

"The last time I was here," Patton said, "you had a special rate for us—spring fever or something."

"It's not spring."

"You don't have specials?"

"So you've been a previous guest," said the man. "Let me look it up," he said, typing. "We have a special return guest rate."

Patton leaned in and whispered, "Except that wasn't my name then. Can't a guy have, you know, secrecy anymore?"

The young man smiled, catching his meaning. "Ah," he said, also in a whisper. "The Amour rate, you might want. How about I call you Harvey Lampan? A Mr. Lampan has that special rate with us."

"That will be just fine," said Patton.

The young man typed it all in and gave him an electronic key card. "Do you have any baggage, Mr. Lampan?"

"Yeah, out front in my…limo. I'll tell the valet he can park it now."

"Very good, Mr. Lampan," said the man. "Enjoy your stay, sir."

Patton's room was spacious. Not only did it have an extra large bed, but also there was a stuffed green chair with a matching ottoman, a round breakfast table, two matching chairs, and a writing desk. The bathroom featured a heart-shaped tub. It was a room that Tess would have loved.

At the desk, he set up his laptop, connecting to the Internet. He searched for the Tosca Café, found it on Columbus Avenue, which was about a dozen blocks south. No point in waiting. He grabbed Chatterley's photo and headed out.

A large neon sign for Tosca loomed when he was a few blocks away. The bar and café were in a two-story building on a quaint street. All streets in the heart of San Francisco were quaint. It was across the street from

City Lights Bookstore, which itself was on the corner of Saroyan Place, and he now remembered going here, talking to Tess about playwright William Saroyan after seeing the street sign. She said she'd once met his poet son, Aram Saroyan, at USC. Aram had written a famous one-word poem: Lighght. Patton hoped for some lighght this very moment.

He stepped through the wood-and-glass doors of the café. It was deep and narrow; the walls, mostly dark wood. Few people were at the stools at the long bar, but the chatter was loud from the people in the red booths and tables at the back. A gray-haired bartender behind the counter poured a light red liquid into the first of three side-by-side martini glasses. Patton stepped up to the man. "Excuse me. I'm looking for a woman who I think used to work here." Patton laid the photo on the bar. Gramps looked at the photo, then back to Patton. "She's pretty. I can see why you're lookin' for her."

"Actually, she was murdered."

"I'm sorry," he said, looking at Patton more closely. "Are you a dick?"

"Pardon?"

The man grimaced. "Sorry. I felt compelled to say that. This place is known for it being film noirish. Basic Instinct was filmed here, you know. So are you a detective?"

"Sure. Do you recognize her?"

The man looked at her more, then shook his head. "I've worked here twenty-five years, and I think I'd remember her if she worked here. Do you know what year?"

"No. Had to be in the last five because she was only in her twenties."

"Let me take this to a few people who've worked here at least five years," and he stepped off. He came back a few minutes later. "Sorry. No one recognizes her. Maybe she was just a customer."

He nodded. Faith had said Chatterley hadn't known much about being a cocktail waitress, and if she'd really worked here, she would have. Still, Patton had hoped this place would give him answers.

"Thanks, anyway," said Patton, pulling his photo back.

"Would you like a drink?" said the bartender. "Looks like you could use one."

"No, I have too much to do. Thanks." As Patton scuffed back to the hotel, a lone saxophonist, dark skin, gray hair, blew quietly on a corner, nothing he recognized but saxophones were a sad instrument. A hat was turned up for donations, and Patton gave him five. As much as Patton was feeling desperate and alone, the saxophonist seemed even sadder.

Back in his room, he took a Starbucks packaged Frappuccino from the minifridge for the caffeine. He had no time to wallow. He jumped online and found all the modeling agencies in San Francisco. He came up with a list of nine large and reputable businesses, as he gathered from a few lists, as well as a half-dozen new or small agencies that did not mask for escort services or other erotic needs. He used Google Maps to find that six of the agencies were within walking distance of Fisherman's Wharf.

He spent the rest of the night watching TV. He forgot to call his mother.

When he went to bed, he pulled back the crisp white sheet, blanket, and bedspread of the bed as large as San Francisco Bay. He slipped in, pulling everything over him neatly like a small splash from underneath the Golden Gate Bridge. He turned his head to the nightstand. A digital clock radio blinked 12:00.

In his dreams, he imagined meeting Tess at the Tosca Café. They hurried to the Pacific Regent, where they undressed. She had a thin frame with medium-sized breasts—a body he could draw for days. Her narrow waist melded into sexy curvaceous hips. He let his hands run over her shoulders, her neck, and to her soft breasts. They made love.

She pulled on her blouse that lay next to the bed. She stood and headed to the bathroom. The crinkling sound of cellophane meant a new toothbrush was being unwrapped. The sound of her brushing vigorously meant she was trying to wash the taste of him out of her mouth. The final sound was of the toothbrush landing in the trash.

CHAPTER 13 (DAY 6)

P atton jerked up in bed to the sounds of a helicopter. Through the window's sheers, the gray day didn't give him a sense of how late it was, and the helicopter whomped past, probably a news helicopter looking at the traffic. What time was it? He felt unusually confused and groggy. How much of the day had burned away? The digital clock radio still blinked 12:00. Patton pressed zero on the phone.

"Front desk" came a male voice.

"Yes, what time is it?"

"Ten oh two, Sir."

"Thank you."

"What time is checkout each day?"

"Eleven a.m. Will you be checking out today?"

"No. Maybe not for two days."

"Very well, Sir."

"Have a good one," Patton said, figuring someone should have a good one. He hung up.

While he wanted to visit each agency and show his photo of Chatterley to see if she was from here, he couldn't do it today. It was Sunday. This and the fact that he wasn't even positive this was her city and that he'd likely go to jail made him feel like the time as a kid when he'd been swinging on a tree branch alone, and his hands slipped. He'd landed on his back, the wind knocked out of him so much that he could barely breathe. He'd thought he was about to die. He struggled right now, too, with his breath. His wife was in trouble and didn't completely trust him. His mother and lawyer were upset, and the Las Vegas police wanted to arrest him and help convict him. The FBI searched for him, too, and here he was in San Francisco looking for a model's history in a haystack. Today might be a good day to stick his head in an oven.

He needed to get out and get some air.

He dressed in sweats, took the elevator down, pushed out the door and ran for the water and wharf. As beautiful as the bay usually was, today he could only smell dead fish. As he jogged down an asphalt path, everyone he passed appeared dour, but maybe it was just him. After passing three different bicycle rental stands, he considered them. A bicycle might be perfect. He could get a sense of speed and see more of the city, perhaps sear away his sense of doom. The Golden Gate Bridge and beyond would make for a good destination. Running back to the last stand, he rented a ten-speed and headed off.

Just down the hill from the old Ghiradelli chocolate factory, as he whizzed past slow-moving bicyclists, two young women on bikes in front of him almost seemed stopped. He was about to shout for them to just walk when they tangled together and fell from their bikes. Patton almost ran into them but shot onto the lawn to the right. One girl must have hit the other from behind. A female roller skater zipped around them on the other side as the girls were groaning in pain. Laying his bike down, Patton ran over. One young woman was small and Asian, and the other was bigger boned and Scandinavian if anything.

"You okay?" he asked.

The Asian woman scooted out from the bikes. She had a t-shirt emblazoned with the word Hawaii. "I should have been looking ahead. Sorry, Michelle," she said to her companion.

The larger woman sat up and brushed her knee. Her t-shirt had a shot of Led Zeppelin's classic first album with a dirigible in flames. "I shouldn't have slowed down. Sorry, Narumi."

Patton helped each woman to her feet and picked up their bikes, single-speeds with baskets on the front. He set them on their kickstands. Pedestrians and bicyclists continued past.

"You're not used to riding?" asked Patton.

"We're from L.A.," said Narumi. "Not much practice."

"You're nice," said the other woman. "I'm Michelle."

"Yes, nice," said Narumi. They held out their hands, and Patton shook them.

"Just be careful," said Patton, turning back to his bicycle.

"Would you like to go to a museum with us? The de Young." They each nodded eagerly.

"Thanks, but I'm headed for the Golden Gate Bridge," he said and pointed.

CHAPTER 13

"The museum's one of the most amazing in America," said Narumi. "And it's in a new building. If you're thinking we're picking up on you, well, we are." They giggled.

"Didn't your mother tell you about strangers?"

"You saved us," said Narumi.

Patton laughed, put his hand to his mouth, but laughed even more.

"What?" asked Michelle.

"No, it's just things are a little tense right now for me, but seeing you two, so open and innocent. It's just funny is all. I'm sorry."

They beamed. "Then you should come with us," said Narumi.

"I can't but I have a favor. My phone's out. May I make a quick call on one of your phones? You have an L.A. number, right?"

Michelle pulled out her iPhone in a pink case. "Yes, use mine."

The fact the call would be from a stranger's phone would be perfect. "Just a couple minutes," he said. He called his mother. She answered after the first ring.

"Mom, it's Patton."

"Where are you?" she said. "Are you in L.A.?"

"I can't say—for your own protection."

"Do you know how upset Brian is?"

He stepped further onto the lawn, away from the girls, so they wouldn't hear. "I'm sorry. I had to do this—the only way to find answers."

"He says there's now a warrant for your arrest and a BOLO for your car."

"I expected that," he said, even if he felt his heart pound again. Maybe he shouldn't have called.

"Brian says he feels like he's watching a friend on the edge of the Golden Gate Bridge, ready to fall."

Patton turned on his heel to see the very Golden Gate Bridge. They couldn't know where he was. It was just coincidence—yet he had to pause to try to calm down.

"I'll call him later. I just didn't want to be jailed. There's too much to do."

"Such as what?"

"I'm doing what the Las Vegas police should be doing—finding the girl's murderer."

"Please," his mother said more softly than he'd expect. "Brian knows what he's doing."

"And I don't?" When she said nothing, he said, "This is the only hope I have. I love you, Mom."

"I love you, too."

Hanging up, he stepped back to the women. "Thank you," he said, returning the phone to Michelle.

"So, are you coming with us to the museum?"

"I'm afraid not," he said, "but thank you, though. You made my day."

When he glided onto the bridge, the gentle breeze made him feel as if he were flying. Coming to this city may have been the stupidest thing he'd done in his life, but he had to appreciate the good things: those girls, his mother, the swooping cables of the bridge. Small moments counted.

Chapter 13

CHAPTER 14 (DAY 7)

On Monday morning, Patton ate breakfast in the sports bar off the lobby, and he appeared at his first agency, the Francesca Bell Agency, before ten a.m. The agency had a much smaller lobby than the agency he'd visited in Las Vegas, but its elegant wood paneling held gorgeous photos of models on magazine covers such as San Francisco, Wine & Spirits, and Curve. He approached the receptionist as if he'd done this a hundred times and said, "I'm investigating the murder of a model in Las Vegas, and I have reason to believe she may have worked here. May I speak with the head of the company?"

The receptionist, stylish and pretty, called instantly and soon walked him to Ms. Bell's office.

"I'm not clear how I might help you," said Ms. Bell, a slender woman in her fifties, who stood and shook his hand.

"I'm looking for the family of a murdered model," Patton explained. He pulled out the short newspaper article from the Las Vegas Review-Journal and showed it to her. "There's reason to believe she worked in San Francisco with a top agency before she moved to Las Vegas."

"Are you with the police?" she asked pleasantly, motioning him to a seat.

"No, I'm a friend."

"And the name of this woman?"

Patton pulled the photo of Chatterley from his briefcase. "The police seem to think she had an alias. I knew her as Chatterley."

"What kind of model was she?" The woman frowned, then took the photo.

"She mostly worked as a product person at conventions."

Ms. Bell took the photo. Her eyebrows went up, as if she recognized her. "Oh. I…her face is familiar, but I can't say why."

"Could she have worked for you?"

"No. I know my former and present models well. For some reason, I'm thinking national—that she's out of New York. Is that possible?"

Patton sighed. What if Chatterley had told the truth, that she'd been from back East? Maybe she'd been a top model out of New York. This would mean he'd have to go to New York. He still had to try all the agencies in San Francisco first. "It's possible," said Patton. "Maybe she worked in New York, then San Francisco."

"I'm sorry. I don't know who she is."

He thanked Ms. Bell and went to his next agency. By 12:30, he'd been to four more agencies, speaking with people who knew past models. None of them recognized Chatterley. One man, however, had asked him, "Why exactly do you think she worked in San Francisco?"

"Her agent in Las Vegas said she was well trained as a model, which would mean working for a top agency in a big city."

"That could happen in Boston—why San Francisco?"

"Her accent, for one. She clearly wasn't from Boston, and she also knew a lot about sourdough bread."

The man gaffawed. "You've got to be kidding me."

"I work with what I got."

"Any bread in particular she liked?" he said, still chuckling.

"Boudin."

"That's good bread. The Boudin bakery and restaurant is on Fisherman's Wharf—and there's a big agency nearby, too, Land O' Talent. Have you been there?"

"It's on my list."

"Good luck," said the man.

Land O' Talent was on the second story of a building a block from the bay. The lobby window offered a postcard view of the marina and the Golden Gate Bridge as well as an angle on a huge blue parking garage with two-story ads for In-and-Out Burger and Hooters.

"Mr. Kleinschmidt will see you now," said the receptionist.

"Thank you."

As they approached the end office, a woman's voice could be heard. "Are you kidding me? This is just like you."

"What do you mean?" said a male voice.

"Never consulting me."

"I consult you all the time. We're consulters."

The receptionist stopped when hearing the voices, and she held out her hand for Patton to wait there. "They're married," the receptionist whispered. She stepped forward and the woman on the other side said, "You'd like to consult with every woman here."

"Stop it already. I have a meeting."

"Another woman?"

There was no audible answer. With a pause in the argument, the receptionist lightly knocked on the door.

"Come in," said the man.

The receptionist opened the door and said, "Are you ready for Mr. Burch?"

"Certainly," said the man. The receptionist motioned Patton forward.

Mr. Kleinschmidt's office offered the same view as the lobby. Mr. Kleinschmidt stood and held out his hand while his wife sat near the window. "Hello, I'm Evan Kleinschmidt," he said. He was a short, chinless man in his forties, with a comb-over. His dark tailored suit showed off his wide shoulders and thin waist. He must have worked out often. They shook hands, as the receptionist left, and Evan said, "And this is my wife, Lillie."

"A pleasure," said his wife, holding out her hand. Slightly taller than him and wearing a tight Nike swoosh shirt and dark pants, she looked as if she'd been a model who, now in her early-thirties, worked out, too. Her biceps were larger than the average woman's, and her firm stance and straight-back shoulders suggested she wouldn't hesitate in kick-boxing her husband.

"I'm sorry if I'm interrupting anything," said Patton.

"Are you kidding me?" said Lillie. "If we don't express how we feel, things fester, right honey?"

Evan nodded.

"Are you married?" Lillie asked.

Patton was still considering the word "fester." Is that what had happened with Tess and him?

"I noticed your ring," she said.

Patton looked up. "I am. Yes. I hope to stay married, too."

"Good," she said, turning to her husband. "You're happy, right?"

"Absolutely," said Evan. "Lillie has an eye for talent, but then she can get a little jealous."

"Hey, he seduced me in this office when I was but twenty. I have to worry every now and then with a guy like this."

Evan grinned like a fat kid whose dream of a candy store had been earned. These two came across as Beauty and the Beast, yet the woman gazed at her flat-faced husband as if he were a rock star. Tess could be that way with him.

Patton said, "I'm looking for the family of a model. There's reason to believe she worked in San Francisco with a top agency before she moved to Las Vegas." When Patton showed Chatterley's photo, the man gasped. "Samantha," they both said.

"What?"

"Samantha Malkey," said Lillie. "She was a wonderful model, and then she returned to Santa Rosa to work at a winery."

"Do you know which one?"

They both shrugged.

"You say she died?" said Evan.

"She may have been murdered."

Lillie sat down slowly. "Why would anyone want to kill her?"

"I don't know," said Patton. "The Las Vegas police didn't know who she was, so her parents don't know she died. Do you have any contact information?"

"Yes, of course." Evan turned to a file drawer nearby and pulled it out. "I knew her fairly well. Her parents I never met."

"Me, neither," said Lillie.

"I remember they had unusual names." Evan pulled out a manila folder, flipped through a few pages, and said, "Ah. Her parents' names are Krzysztof and Wilhelmina."

"German?"

"I guess so. I should know these things with my name, but I don't. They live in Santa Rosa, about an hour from here." He showed the address and phone number for her parents, which Patton copied down.

Patton thanked Evan and Lillie who, standing together, now seemed pleased with each other as if they'd just funded a new hospital wing. As Patton left, the couple hugged and kissed. Patton didn't feel envious. The feeling was more like hope.

He returned to his hotel, and as he walked, he felt excited, and he jumped up and punched the air. So what if it was just after one p.m. and he'd missed checkout time but still needed to leave. The extra cost was well worth the information he just received. He needed to call Brian when he got to his room.

He packed quickly. The bed had already been made up, and he sat on it and picked up the phone. He called Brian's office and told the secretary who he was.

"Patton!" Brian said immediately picking up. "Where are you? Do you know how much trouble you're in?"

"It's worth it," said Patton. "Am I still your client?"

"Your mother made sure of that."

"I found out Chatterley's real name, Samantha Malkey. I'm on my way to see her parents, I hope. Don't you think this changes everything?"

"Maybe. Maybe not if there's no evidence of anyone after her."

"And why would she change names?"

"So, where are you?"

"There's client-attorney privilege, right?"

"Of course."

"San Francisco. I'm headed to Santa Rosa. How much trouble am I in?"

"There's a warrant for your arrest, and you're on Nevada's most wanted list. California's alerted. If you have a traffic stop, you're likely to be arrested and extradited. Even if you're found innocent of all charges later, you could be prosecuted for evading arrest."

"They never do that on Law and Order."

"You pissed off some cops. This isn't Law and Order."

"So, what would you like me to do? Stop now and go to Nevada?"

"Let me send my P.I. to Santa Rosa, and, yes, come back. I can make another deal with Las Vegas Metro."

"I can't, Brian. I'm following this through."

Brian gave an audible sigh. "Your wife called."

Patton leaned forward, pressed the phone to his ear. "Did you talk to her?"

"Yes."

"Is she still in L.A.? Did she leave a phone number again?"

"She left nothing, really said nothing except that she's been going over Birnam's emails looking for clues."

"Did she find any?"

"She didn't say."

"What're we supposed to do?"

"She said she'd call back to get your phone number."

"I have to check in somewhere first. Can't you make a deal with the FBI for her? She was swindled."

"I'll talk with her when she calls. Call me when you have a new number."

"All right."

"Listen. Be careful. If you really are on the murderer's trail, he's already killed at least twice. Let my P.I. do it."

"I'll be careful."

Before leaving the room, Patton used the Internet for directions to Santa Rosa. There was the scenic route and the freeway route, the latter being faster. He needed to see the Malkeys as soon as possible. He considered calling them, but he couldn't risk their disappearance in case one of them had anything to do with their daughter's death. Seeing how they reacted to the news in person might reveal a lot.

Patton checked out and was soon on the road.

He crossed the Golden Gate Bridge, its elegant reddish cables draping on either side of him. Over the next hour, he passed picturesque Sausalito, zoomed by Petaluma, and headed into Santa Rosa. Following the map to the address, he took the Highway 12 East exit. The highway ended in a couple miles at Farmer's Lane, where there was a Starbucks coffee shop down to the right. He proceeded straight onto Hoen, and soon found the Malkey house on a corner of a side street. The yellow boxy house had artichokes growing at the curbside, a small green lawn, and a flowerbed near the front door with rosemary and tomato plants.

He rang the doorbell, and a large dog barked. Its tapping feet ran to the door where the dog's bark was even louder. "Christ, shut-up already," said a man's voice, and soon the door opened to a man in jeans and black T-shirt. His gray-bearded face looked much like the Gorton's fisherman. "Listen, if it's the Awake and Watchtower again, we don't believe in that shit," the man said.

"Krzysztof Malkey?" said Patton.

"Depends who's talkin'." The dog barked again. "Shut up!" said the man forcefully to the beast, a German Shepherd, which shut up instantly and lay down.

"I'm Patton Burch, a friend of your daughter."

The man resized Patton with some alarm. "She's only in high school. What do you mean, 'friend'?"

"Your daughter, Samantha. I hired her in Las Vegas."

"Samantha?" came a female voice around the corner, and a chair scuttled.

"Stay there, woman," said Mr. Malkey, but a tall thin woman with frizzy gray hair hurried to the door. "Where is she?"

Patton realized neither one had a Germanic accent. Maybe they were second-generation Germans. "As I was saying, I hired your daughter."

"Doing what?"

"I have a bug company. Beneficial bugs."

"What?" said Mr. Malkey.

"Instead of using agricultural chemicals to keep away garden pests, I have good bugs."

"What was Sam doing for you?" he said with impatience.

"Helping out in my booth at a convention in Las Vegas. We hired her—my wife and I—from a modeling agency."

They both stared at him as if waiting for why he came.

"I take it no one from Las Vegas has called you?" he said.

The woman looked worried. "No," she said.

"Ah… well…" He took a deep breath. There was no easy way to say this. He pulled out the short newspaper article from the Las Vegas Re-view-Journal and handed it to her. "Samantha died," said Patton, and the woman's eyes widened and her face crinkled. "From asthma complications," he added.

The woman barely breathed out a "No" as she fell against her husband, grasping him.

Mr. Malkey seemed surprised, slow to hold his wife. "I don't under-stand," he said. "Why is it you who's telling us?"

"Your daughter was using a different name—I'm not clear why—and the police said the coroner was responsible for finding her relatives, which might take weeks or longer—if ever. I thought I'd find you faster."

Mrs. Malkey sobbed into her husband's shirt. This was exactly the fear Patton had about having children. If they died before you, how could you go on?

"I only knew your daughter a short time, but I really liked her. I didn't want her buried as a Jane Doe. She had to be someone. I then learned she was your daughter, Samantha. I'm so sorry."

"Bless you," Mrs. Malkey breathed. Mr. Malkey just stared at him.

"So you haven't heard from her in a while?" Patton asked.

"Where's her body?" said Mr. Malkey. "Am I supposed to pay some-thing? Is that what this is about?"

His wife hit him in the chest.

"The coroner I'm sure has her still," said Patton. "If you go there and identify her, and have some proof she's your daughter, I'm sure they'll re-lease her—I'm so sorry." He could only think how horrible this would be if some stranger came to the door to tell the news. He could hardly speak now, but he eeked out, "Maybe you should call first."

"Come in, come in," the woman said, straightening up, still sniffling.

"I'm Willi—Wilhelmina. And this is Kris. We want to know all about her."
She handed the article back to him.

"She did this to spite me," said Kris.

"She did not," said Willi. "She didn't leave because she was mad at
you."

"Then why'd she leave?" Kris just shook his head. Patton knew from
the cookbook that Samantha had had issues with her father. He could get
mad.

They guided him into the living room, passing the door to the galley
kitchen, which had a breakfast table at the far end, near sliding glass doors
to the outside. The backyard, shallow with six-foot cinder block walls,
looked overgrown and weedy. He wondered had it been as neglected when
Samantha played there as a child?

Willi pointed for Patton to sit in the one stuffed armchair. Kris didn't
look happy about that, but he sat with his wife on the well-worn beige
couch.

"We hadn't heard from Sam in over a year, ever since we received a
postcard saying she'd be gone a while."

"To where?" said Patton.

"She didn't say," Kris said.

"I always thought her asthma might do her in," Willi said. "I should
have breast fed her when she was a baby."

"Stop it," said Kris. "It's nothing you did. She's responsible for everything she's done."

"Not asthma."

"Did she live with you?" Patton asked.

"She moved out at sixteen," said Kris.

"You kind of made her move," said Willi.

Kris slapped her knee. "We are not rehashing history. This man, thank
you very much," he said nodding to Patton, "came here to give us some
information. If we can get that coroner's number from you, we won't keep
you any longer." Kris stood. The man stared at the floor, looking sad and
deep in thought.

Patton stood to be polite, but he didn't want to go. "I'm sorry to be the
bearer of bad news."

"And I'm sorry she's dead, and… And I have regrets. You ever have
regrets, Mr. Patton?"

"Burch. Patton Burch. Yes, I have regrets."

"There you have it."

Patton nodded but didn't know what he had. He needed to know more. "There's something else about her passing," he said. "It doesn't say in the article, but the Las Vegas police think she was murdered."

"What?" said Kris.

"You said she died of asthma," said Willi. By the look on her face, this appeared to be even worse information.

"Someone purposely put ragweed pollen in her inhaler, which did her in. Can you think of anyone who wanted her gone—anyone who knew she had asthma?" Patton sat back down.

Willi tugged her husband back down and looked at him for help.

"She was fucking murdered?" He stood again. "Who? Who did this?" He looked like he was ready to beat him up.

"I don't know," said Patton. "I wish I did."

Kris sat, deflated, and shook his head slowly as if still thinking of possibilities. "She was a good girl. Everyone liked her."

"Yes," said Willi. "And she did just fine at the winery, too. Once she got a job there, we became close again, saw her often."

"I don't get it," said Kris. "Murdered?"

"The postcard you mentioned," Patton said. This seemed a key piece of evidence. "What did you do after you received it?"

"Do?" said Kris.

"I'm sorry."

"She was an adult. Were we to hire a private detective to drag her home? Hire a psychologist to tell us what we did wrong in raising her?" He glared at Patton.

Patton nodded. "I'd be as frustrated in your position."

"I called some of her friends," said Willi, "to see if they knew anything, but they got cards, too."

Patton wanted her list of friends, but he had to earn their trust first. "Do you have your postcard?" Patton asked. "Just curious."

Willi leapt up and headed toward the fireplace, whose mantel held a single postcard as well as candlesticks and little glass and porcelain animals, the kind Samantha had collected. Willi gave Patton the postcard. On the front, the Golden Gate Bridge, bathed in sunlight, stood above a bank of clouds as if the bridge floated in heaven. The backside had a San Francisco postmark, dated thirteen months earlier. The note said, "Dear Mom and Dad. I can't explain now, but I wanted you to know, you won't hear from me for a while. I had to leave quickly. I'll explain another time—I don't want you to know too much right now. Love, Sam."

As he stared at Samantha's handwriting, he wondered why she needed to be so desperate to cut all ties to her family and friends. He remembered her explaining how her fiancé had a sense of violence about him. "Was she engaged?"

"I never saw her date after about age twenty-one," said Willi. "She said she was tired of relationships—they take too much work."

"Too much work?" said Kris.

"Anyway, I'd hoped she'd eloped. She seemed happier the last year. I thought she was dating someone, but she wouldn't say."

"Where was she working just before she suddenly left?" Patton asked.

"She had a perfectly good job at a winery," said Kris, "where she was moving up in the ranks."

"She was giving it up to go to junior college," said Willi. "Kris told her she was too old for that."

"Can I tell my own story?" he asked.

"Go ahead," she said.

"Stick with the winery, I said. She said no. I said okay. It's your life." Kris raised his hands to show that was that.

"Which winery?"

"Naeper."

The front door then opened and closed. A young woman walked in and stood at the edge of the living room. Patton involuntarily jerked when he saw she was a smaller, younger version of Samantha, with the same dark shoulder-length hair, the same innocent oval face and elegant nose. They were sisters. She wore a white blouse and a knee-length checkered skirt.

"This is Emily," said Kris. "This man here is…"

"Patton Burch," he said to Emily, standing, holding out his hand. "I'm in the organic bug business."

"Whatever," Emily said, shaking his hand.

"Why don't you do your homework, dear?"

Patton saw they weren't going to tell her about Samantha now.

"All right," said Emily.

She stared at Patton with a frown, as if she knew something serious was going on. She turned on her heel and strode down the hallway into a bedroom. The door closed. Then it opened a crack. Patton returned to his chair.

"She's a teenager," Willi said.

"I gathered." Patton knew he couldn't take much more of their time, so he quickly tried to think of other things to ask. It seemed clear to him Kris had nothing to do with Samantha's demise. On the TV show Columbo, Peter Falk's character always asked a tough question as he was leaving a scene as if the question had just occurred to him. Patton turned at the door. "You mentioned that Samantha had moved out at sixteen. I'm not clear why."

"That has nothing to do why she was murdered." Kris glared at him.

"If it had something to do outside your family, maybe it did."

"No."

Willi quickly stretched out her hand. "Thank you for coming, Mr. Burch." They shook hands. Kris didn't offer his.

As Patton walked to his van, he thought about what he now had. Something in this town had caused Samantha to flee. She was working at the Naeper Winery, about to leave it for junior college, when she left the area altogether. Why? Her mother had said she was happy, and then Samantha had to suddenly leave?

Before Patton went to the Naeper Winery, he needed to research it. The afternoon still held a couple of hours. He'd go to the Starbucks for the Wifi. As he started his van, a bang on his hood startled him. He looked up to see Emily, her hand on his hood. She ran to his window.

"Mr. Burch," she said. "Samantha… was really murdered?"

"I'm sorry … Yes, she was."

Her eyes welled, and a teardrop fell.

"I'm sorry."

"Have you talked with her fiancé?"

"Your parents said she didn't even have a boyfriend."

"They're clueless. She was basically living with her boyfriend."

"Who?"

"Odell Naeper. You know the Naeper Winery?"

"No." But he thought he soon would.

"Just beyond Kenwood, near here. Their wine is some of the best. Odell runs the place."

"And you suspect him?"

"He was upset when he couldn't find her after she left."

"Did she tell you anything about why she had to leave?"

"No, but the night before she left, she tapped on my window to say good-bye. She looked really scared, shaking even."

"Did she say her fiancé did something?"

"No, but I never liked the guy. He was always, like, trying to help me when I didn't want it."

"And you didn't tell your parents about him?"

"She made me promise not to say anything. Ever."

"And you haven't for all this time? What else did she tell you?"

"That she loved me, and she'd explain everything to me the next time she saw me."

"That's the last you heard of her?"

"Yes."

She looked at him so honestly, so openly, as if he could fix everything. "I'm curious," he said. "Why did your sister move out at sixteen?"

"I was only six then," she said.

"So you don't know?"

"No, she told me later. She said Dad's best friend, who was over for Thanksgiving dinner, came from behind her and grabbed her breasts. He tried kissing her, too. When Sam later told my parents, it caused a big fight. Dad didn't believe her. So she moved out. She was already working as a model then, anyway."

"And what's the name of this friend?"

"I don't know," she said. "Mom said Dad stopped being friends with him. I guess Dad believed Sam after all."

Patton nodded. "Well, thanks for telling me these things."

"You're a detective, right?"

"Actually, I'm not."

She looked puzzled. "But all those questions?"

"I want justice."

"Good." She nodded. "Me, too."

CHAPTER 14

CHAPTER 15

With his Caramel Frappuccino in hand at Starbucks and walking to a table with his laptop in its case, Patton looked for the nearest plug. His laptop was out of a charge. An available plug was next to a young couple at a table. The short-haired man, perhaps a freshman in college looked like a Wally—no particular reason, but he appeared Wallyesque, wearing a plain black t-shirt. Wally stared at the ground as the woman spoke in a serious whisper.

"Mind if I use the plug?" said Patton to the couple.

The woman, pale skin, bright red lipstick, looked up as if he'd asked, "What's your favorite cheese after sex?" She frowned, saw his laptop, then nodded. She seemed like a Natasha to him—a well-grounded Russian with a tiny heart. Patton kneeled and plugged in the cord.

"What am I supposed to do?" said Wally.

Patton realized the young man was talking to Natasha. She didn't say anything, and Patton sensed he was in their way.

"Thanks," said Patton. "Sorry."

Wally stared down, and Patton could empathize. They seemed to be breaking up.

Patton fiddled with the cord. It was long enough that most of it lay on the ground and wouldn't trip anyone. Natasha whispered something, and Patton purposely angled himself away so he wouldn't be looking at them. Give them their privacy. Still, their sorrow blew as a hot wind. Happiness always felt the same, but sadness had a stronger radiation, a blackness that burned.

Their plight, of course, made him think of Tess. Where might she be now? Maybe she was in a coffee shop and they were living parallel lives.

Patton used Google to search for "Naeper Winery." He soon learned it was on 240 acres just off of Highway 12 on the other side of Glen Ellen and stretched from the valley floor up into the hills. The vineyard had a long list of awards from California State Fairs, Sonoma County Harvest Fairs, the San Francisco Chronicle's annual wine competition, and various national and international competitions.

There was a photo of the Naeper tasting room, a white clapboard house made from the remnants of the original house where Wells Fargo stagecoaches stopped to water their horses on the way from Santa Rosa to Sonoma. Rather than a shack, though, it looked like a small version of a home on Desperate Housewives' Wisteria Lane—hard to imagine horses stopping here 140 years ago.

When he clicked on "About Us," up came a photo of a blond-haired man in his mid-forties, blue blazer, red tie, looking handsome and assured. The text said, "Odell Naeper, proprietor of the Naeper Winery, is the grandson of legendary founder H.R. Naeper, an adventurer who came to the Valley of the Moon on his way to Alaska just before World War I and fell in love with the place. He began the winery on just nine acres."

The next paragraphs gave a history of how Naeper befriended and listened to his neighbor, author Jack London, on the use of terracing and manure spreading, techniques London used on his Beauty Ranch in nearby Glen Ellen. Naeper bought more land, and the legend of his wines grew.

Odell was the fourth child of H.R.'s son, Gerald. Gerald had taken over the vineyard in 1960 after the death of his father, and Odell moved up the ranks of the vineyard in the eighties and took over in the mid-nineties after Gerald died at the age of seventy. The last line was, "Odell was voted as one of People magazine's 'Most Eligible Bachelors' last year. He remains so."

The fact that information was on the company's website made Patton guess that Odell probably received plenty of email from women who were interested in a handsome, rich, and eligible man. He probably was a player. Maybe he had just played with Samantha. Why marry if you had people throwing themselves at you?

Patton quickly wrote notes about Odell in his investigative file. While he was handwriting the address to the winery, he heard Natasha tell Wally, "I still want to be your friend."

"No!" said the young man and in one quick motion, the chair scraped back, the wire caught on the boy's foot, and Patton's computer flew off the table. Patton's hands instinctively shot out, but he missed his computer. It clattered to the floor and the screen cracked and flashed off.

"No," Patton gasped.

The boy looked absolutely aghast, near tears, as he looked at Patton, and he said, "I'm sorry. I'm sorry, okay?" He turned to his now-ex-girlfriend and said much louder, "I'm sorry about everything," and then he ran out.

The young woman knelt with Patton on the floor, trying to hand him the now disconnected cord. "Maybe it still works," she said, but Patton could see it didn't.

He took the cord from her hands and said, "It'll be okay." He meant her life, but she pointed to his laptop.

"Do you have insurance?"

"Who has insurance for these things?"

"I know," she said and sat back down, forlorn. She covered her face in her hands.

Patton wanted to say something, but didn't know what. He realized this was how he was with Tess, too, when she was upset. He always wanted to say something, but knew he wasn't good at it, so he'd say nothing.

He also realized all the things he needed to research in the next few days were fucked. Maybe he could find an Internet café. He couldn't buy another computer with his credit card because law officials might be scanning his accounts regularly. He didn't have the Internet on his cell phone, either, and he still wasn't using his cell phone. There might be a good public library.

Patton packed up his laptop, for all the good it did, and carefully wrapped up his charger, too. The young woman looked up. He nodded to her, offered a smile. She nodded back as if to say, "This is life." He left.

At least he had Naeper's address.

— ❀ —

As Patton drove under the wrought-iron arch wrapped in grape vines, a sign said "Naeper Winery Tasting Room." The white clapboard house and a parking lot lay just ahead.

The driveway forked to the left with a sign that said "Deliveries Only," and it went up a hill, at the top of which stood a chateau, a wide and huge two-story pinkish building with French windows and a steep slate roof with several dormers. That's where he wanted to go. Odell wasn't likely to spend his time at the tasting room.

The drive kept winding back and forth up the hill. Patton felt his stomach fall but not because of all the turns. Odell Naeper was a major businessman who had to outfox his siblings to run the place, and he had to be brilliant enough to build the empire further. If Naeper was the person to kill Samantha, he'd be outright ruthless.

The sun, still high enough in the sky, gave a hard light with sharp shadows on the building. One end of the chateau had a round tower with a pointy-hat roof as if it had been inspired by the Hogwarts School of Witchcraft and Wizardry.

The drive was particularly steep just before the top, and he thought how a road like this could not exist in places where it snowed. No car would ever get up it and would probably slip off the edge down the steep rocky hill. There were no rows of vines on that steep section.

The drive flattened out and led to a front circle with a water fountain of nymphs spitting. The marble front stairs led to a double doorway with stained glass. Patton parked his van in front and went up the stairs. He carried his computer in its padded case with its strap over his shoulder. He figured it made him look more legitimate. A sign simply said "Naeper Winery." So he entered. The front room had a woman behind a large oak desk on a light blond parquet floor. The woman, older with gray cropped hair, sat in her straight-backed chair and reminded Patton of Miss Moneypenny in 007 movies.

"I came to see Odell Naeper, if I may," said Patton.

"Do you have an appointment?"

"I don't. My name is Patton Burch—Burch as in birch tree but spelled with a U instead of an I. I'm investigating a young woman he knows, a Ms. Samantha Malkey."

The woman's eyes widened in recognition.

"Do you know her?" Patton asked.

"I'm not his social secretary," she said.

"Would you mind relaying him the message?"

"Please have a seat." She pointed to one of two straight-backed chairs in the corner.

"Thanks."

She pressed a button on her phone and soon said, "Yes, I have a Detective Burch here, like birch tree, inquiring about a Ms. Samantha Malkey." She listened to the response, and said, "I'm not sure… Yes, I'd be happy to." She turned to Patton. "He'll see you in a few minutes. Have a seat."

"Thanks." He remained standing, needing all the energy and self-assurance he could muster. He noted the black picture frames on the wall and moved closer to one to look at what appeared to be a label. It was. The label featured an etching of the very building he was in, and below the large word "Naeper" were the words "Syrah 2006, Bella Vineyard, Sonoma Valley." Next to it in the frame, a gold medallion had been mounted on which said "Indy Gold – International Wine Competition." Now he noticed most of the frames had award medals. Impressive.

Patton turned to gaze out the large picture window by the chairs. The incredible view and the elegance of the front entryway, he realized, was meant to make visitors feel as if they were visiting the gods on Mt. Olympus.

He gazed down the hill to see where he'd been. After he'd left the outskirts of Santa Rosa, the streets and planned community housing gave way to countryside. A sign soon proclaimed, "Valley of the Moon Scenic Drive." Indeed, the two-lane blacktop had wound under oak stands, and vast vineyards beyond the trees blended up into the hills on either side of the highway. Now, from the picture window, Highway 12 looked like a thread of licorice when the broccoli sprigs of trees didn't hide it. The hills themselves looked like a rumpled brown and green quilt—the brown from the stark hillsides, and the green from where grapes grew in tightly knit rows.

Patton turned to the woman at the desk. "You must love coming to work everyday to see this view."

"Yes," she said, "I feel lucky." She turned back to her computer screen to keep working.

"Have you worked here long?"

She stared at him as if he were a Hare Krishna at the door. She said, "You may go up the stairs, turn left, fourth door on the right."

"Oh. Thanks."

Only then did her phone buzz, and she spoke into it: "He's on his way."

The wide staircase was covered in Berber carpeting and featured wrought-iron hand railings. It led to a landing of the same parquet floor as below. On the floor lay a Persian rug in beige and blue, and on the wainscoted wall hung a classic oil painting. A man with a huge white mustache stared down at Patton. The eyes felt alive, spooky, as if daring Patton to step further. Based on the old-fashioned clothes, Patton guessed the portrait to be H.R. Naeper.

Patton took the hallway to the left, feeling anxious but telling himself, steady, steady. Odell Naeper walked toward him, tall, assured, grinning, like any head of state might, softened by wavy blond hair and a scar just under his chin. Patton didn't remember the scar on the website's portrait. Maybe it had been Photoshopped out.

"I'm Patton Burch," he said, holding out his hand.

"Odell Naeper." Wearing a form-fitting blue blazer, Odell shook his hand. "Welcome to the Casa." He said this as if implying it was an unpretentious cozy cottage.

"A beautiful place you have here."

"My father's legacy, actually. My grandfather, H.R., had lived below in what's now the tasting room. This building isn't all house. A lot of the winery's in here—and we rent it out for weddings and things. But you're not here for a rental."

"No. I've been investigating Samantha Malkey."

"I hope she didn't get into trouble. Maybe she's a bit crazy, but she's a good person. I believed in her for a while."

"What do you mean?"

"She left the winery so quickly—never heard from her again except for a postcard."

Patton didn't want to deliver the news while they were walking because he wanted to see Odell's face for a reaction. "Her sister Emily said you were her boyfriend."

"Yes. Come on into the library," said Odell. "And you're investigating what exactly?"

"The circumstances of her departure. Emily said Samantha was more than your girlfriend—that you were engaged?"

"Why would you investigate her departure?"

"Samantha ended up going to Las Vegas and starting a life with a new identity there. I'm trying to find out why."

"I'd love to know, too—but why do you care?"

"Because she was murdered."

It was as if Patton had punched him in the stomach because Odell staggered back and hit the wall. His face crumpled in shock, and his eyes filled with tears.

Patton stepped back. Odell's reaction was more extreme than Samantha's parents. Was it real?

"Why?" Odell whispered.

"That's what I'm trying to figure out, as well as who? You knew her. Maybe you can help."

Odell nodded, wiping his tears. He straighted as best he could and pointed to the open doorway near them. "Let's go in here."

Patton followed Odell. The room had gas logs burning in the fireplace despite it being May. Across the vast room and near two orderly bookcases, a large oak desk held a vase of red roses.

They headed to a sitting area in front of the fireplace. An antique

French-style couch was winged by a stuffed chair on one side and a love-seat on the other. Another Persian rug lay in the middle.

"If you don't mind, I'll ask a few questions, and then I can explain more. You were engaged?" Patton was about to take the loveseat when Odell motioned for him to sit on the much larger couch, which Patton knew would dwarf him. He sat on the end closest to Odell's chair and placed his laptop computer in its padded case on the floor.

"I was engaged, but not many people knew that. Samantha wanted to save the surprise for a party. Then, wham, she was gone. It threw me for a loop, believe me. I mean, don't you think love is the blood in our veins, the wine of our glasses?

"I suppose."

"To quote Dr. Seuss, 'When you're in love, you can't fall asleep because reality is better than your dreams'."

"He didn't make it rhyme?"

Odell laughed. "Why spend the time? Dr. Suess was in love."

"It's a good time of life. Maybe it's why we exist."

"Don't get me wrong," said Odell. "I'm someone who held off marriage for the longest time. But with Samantha, I wanted marriage. She was incredible."

"How so?"

"Loving, loyal, gorgeous, funny." He smiled wide, back in the moment.

"Loyal until the day she left, you mean?"

Odell looked crushed. He nodded. "Marriage means commitment. Of course, so does insanity." His smile broke through. "And I felt insane for a while after she left. But then I eventually fell in love with someone else. I'm married now."

"Your website said differently."

"I know, I've got to change that." He picked up a silver picture frame on the end table between them and handed it to Patton. The photo showed Odell in a tux hugging a woman in a wedding dress. She looked mousy—none of the allure of Samantha.

"Are you married, Detective?"

"Yes." Patton was off-balance for a second. "I think."

"You don't know?"

"The ups and downs of marriage, right?"

Odell shrugged, then said, "You know, I'm new at it, so most of the time I feel like an orangutan trying to learn the violin. As Martin Heidegger might say, I'm thrown—geworfenheit was his word."

"Heidegger?"

"A German philosopher. It's good to be thrown. Keeps you on your toes. We should be thrown every day of our lives."

Patton nodded but had no idea what he meant. He had the uneasy feeling Odell was trying to throw him, though.

"I'd like a son to take this all on," said Odell.

"Not a daughter?"

Odell paused as if thinking. "Girls are aligned with their mothers, don't you think?"

"I don't know. I don't have kids."

"It's not too late, right?" Odell clapped Patton on the back. "Isn't that why we're here?"

"To procreate?" He shrugged, and Odell chuckled.

"You're all right, guy," Odell said. "I'll tell you after my wife delivers."

"When's she due?"

"Four months."

Patton smiled, but he had to remember this guy might be a murderer.

"As far as Samantha," said Odell, "are you with the, what, the Las Vegas police?"

"No, no. I'm doing this independently." Patton hoped that sounded like he was a private detective.

"Who hired you? Her family? What is it you're doing independently?"

"When the police couldn't find her real identity, I decided to help out. She deserves a proper burial or cremation. I found she's from Santa Rosa. I was able to find her parents, and after I learned about you, I thought you should know, too."

Odell straightened in his chair, regaining his composure. "Thank you." He stared now at Patton as if he were analyzing every cell. "What was Samantha doing in Las Vegas exactly?

"I knew Samantha by a different name, Chatterley Langstrump."

"Chatterley Langstrump?" The way he pronounced the name made it seem absurd. "And how did you know her?"

"I was her last employer."

Odell blinked a few times.

Patton added, "I'm in the beneficial bug business. I have a company."

Odell looked bewildered. "So you're a businessman who, through the kindness of his heart, hunted down Samantha's identity so you could give her parents and me the news?"

"Yes, basically."

Odell looked skeptical.

Patton reached for his wallet and pulled out a BenBugs card. "Here's my business."

Odell looked at it carefully. "President. BenBugs," he said.

"Yes. It's all about going organic. Beneficial bugs instead of chemicals. Have you considered going organic?"

"So this is a business call?"

"No. I liked Samantha, and the police weren't finding out who she was."

Odell placed his card in his wallet.

"She was a lovely person, completely," said Patton. "When was the last time you saw her?" Patton tried to make it sound innocuous and merely curious.

Odell said nothing for at least a minute, hunched. "I'm so sad about this. I feel blindsided—sorry."

"That's okay."

"Thank you for coming." Odell stood, his hand out. "I'll take you at your word—you're doing this to be kind." They shook.

Patton had so much more to ask, but clearly this was over. With nothing to lose, he said, "If you don't mind my asking, where were you six days ago?"

Odell glared at him in disbelief, pulling back his hand. "What are you suggesting? You're not even a cop. Were you in love with her, is that it?"

"No."

"What the fuck are you doing? You show up unannounced."

"I'm sorry. I'm just trying to tell the people who knew her."

"So you're just doing a good thing?" Odell smirked. "Who does just good things?"

"Lots of people. Samantha did."

"I wonder." He shook his head. "The only way I can rationalize why she left was that she was a model who knew how to use her face and body. She must have found a richer guy."

"She didn't. She was nearly broke and was attending a community college," Patton said.

"We have a perfectly good college here. Why Las Vegas?"

"Something happened to make her leave here in a hurry."

"Which makes me more puzzled than ever. But I hope I'm not under suspicion by a bug man."

Patton stared right back at the man, holding his ground. "I'm not a cop or a private eye, true—doesn't mean I'm not doing the right thing. Someone put pollen in her inhaler—killed her—which means someone knew about her allergies."

"I knew about her allergies."

"Exactly."

Odell laughed. "So do you now put me under organic questioning or something?"

Patton stood. "I'm sorry to take your time. Don't be mad at the messenger."

"I hate you going away suspicious, even if you're not the law. Tell you what," said Odell. "Let me open my doors metaphorically. I have an appointment, but let me introduce you to June LeCompte, my personal secretary, who will tell you anything you want to know about me, such as I was here last week. You can learn about the winery. You'll even get a bottle of our best. Will that be okay for you?"

He knew Odell was merely humoring him, but he'd take any opening he could get. "Yes. Thanks. More than okay."

As they walked down the stairs, Odell said, "Is there anything I can do to help Samantha's parents?"

"Such as what?" They stepped down a hallway.

"Maybe I could help pay for her funeral. I'd been in love with her, after all."

Here was another opening for Patton. "Did you know them, her parents?"

"Not really."

"Ah."

"I still don't get you," said Odell. "You're the citizen investigator?"

They arrived at an office. Outside the double French doors, the office had a nameplate on the outside, "June LeCompte, Executive Assistant." Through the small panes, Patton saw she was on the phone looking at her flat-panel computer screen. Odell tapped on one of the panes with a big smile and opened the door.

"Speak of the devil," said June with a big grin and wink to her boss. Gorgeous, with thick red hair to her shoulders, she was nodding to her unseen caller. "Anyway, the bottling's going great—more cases than ever," June said in what sounded to be a British accent. "We've got Kenwood and Cohn beat together. Got to go. Ta ta."

As he stepped in, Patton jerked as he saw a big black long-eared dog in the corner, and on a second look, he realized it was a big stuffed one, the kind one might win at a state fair for some impossible task.

She hung up and sprung from her seat. "That cheeky bastard always makes me smile—Waverly."

"He ask you on a date yet?" said Odell.

"He's a piker," she said, and gave a wink, this time to Patton, then pointing to her dog. "I saw you flinch. Real looking isn't it? My daughter bought that at a toy store in Point Reyes. Of course she's too old for it now, but it makes the perfect pet—or husband. Nothing to do."

"You're British?" Patton asked.

"Kiwi," she said. "New Zealand."

"June, this is Patton Burch, as in tree."

"With a U, not an I," said Patton.

"He's an investigator with a bit of sad news." That had her attention. "Our Samantha was murdered in Las Vegas."

June's mouth dropped, her hand came to her chest, and she, too, looked hurt by the news. "I'm so sorry, Odell." She looked at Patton. "I knew her, too. A very sweet girl. Do you know why she left here so suddenly? Is that what brings you here?"

Patton was about to say something when Odell said, "Yes. He's trying to learn more about Samantha and about my relationship to her."

"Oh," she said, more somberly.

"Please help Mr. Burch out with any questions about Samantha or me. Even give him a tour, if he likes. Does that sound good, detective?"

He looked at Odell with a nod, liking how Odell's calling him "detective" gave him credibility with June. "Yes, that's wonderful. Thank you."

"Anyway, June, I've got a meeting. See you later. Maybe I won't see you again, Mr. Burch, so thank you for updating us." He shook Patton's hand firmly.

Patton realized Odell Naeper might be arrogant, but he was also well-liked and bold. If Odell wasn't involved, this would put Patton back at square one.

June turned off her screen and said, "How about a terroir tour?"

He shrugged and nodded, not really knowing what he was agreeing to. Anything was fine.

"Terroir is a term that means 'sense of place.' I'll give you a sense of place—indoors and out."

"Wonderful."

For the next thirty minutes, June spun off a lot of facts as she took him into many of the backrooms. He slipped in questions about Samantha and Odell's relationship. How did they meet? Were they really in love? How did Odell propose? And more. June made Samantha and Odell's story seem like Prince Rainer of Monaco meets movie star Grace Kelly—an epic, romantic, destined thing that ended when Samantha disappeared for no clear reason.

"So he never heard from her again?" he asked.

"No. He was so crushed, I'd never seen him like that. After about a month he threw himself into the business, nothing else."

"So how did he meet the woman he married?"

"At a wine tasting. Once they started dating, it was as if he was determined to put everything with Samantha behind him. We never talked about her again until today."

Nothing still made sense to Patton. Maybe if he focused on what June was showing him of the winery, if he could see what Odell ran, maybe he'd understand him more. One room had many casks stacked on racks. Some of these casks had wine that was properly aged, so they were being bottled now in another area. Another room looked like a chemistry lab with stainless steel tables and high-tech machines that analyzed wine. A bottling room, in full operation, needed only four employees who could bottle up to twenty-four thousand bottles per day. Bottling did not happen every day. One of the men, a short Hispanic-looking man in his early forties with slicked-back black hair and a graying goatee, waved to June, then dumped corks into a bin. "Twelve bottles to a case," said June, "which comes to two thousand cases a day."

"You grow that many grapes to bottle so much?"

"Like most wineries, we grow some and buy grapes from many independent vineyards. We use the 'cuvée' winemaking method. The harvest from each vineyard is handled separately to preserve its individuality and true character. We're aiming for a hundred thousand cases this year."

She led him outside to the back slate patio, which was now in shadow so late in the day. While the front view was gone, the hillside held neat row after row of vines in terracing that gently rose above him. The rows continued down the hill on either side of the winery like foam spilling from a cappuccino. Patton walked to what appeared to be a square of sod on the slate. A golf tee stuck up from the artificial turf.

As if anticipating his question, June said, "Odell loves to drive a bucket of golf balls into the vineyard most nights."

"Doesn't it hurt the grapes?"

"Not enough to matter."

Patton gazed out, imagining where two-hundred yards would be— still in a flat area. "This has to be the ultimate in ownership: a vineyard as your driving range."

"The workers collect the balls every morning."

June brought him down the steps, and they headed toward the nearest row. Now that they were close, Patton saw just how thickly the vines grew on wires, like ivy on a wall. "Beautiful," he said. "If it were mine, I'd do anything to keep it."

"It's still spring," June said, "so the leaves are still coming." She didn't seem to notice his insinuation. Rather, she held her arms out, closed her eyes, and breathed in deeply. "The air is wine. Across Sonoma Mountain, wisps of sea fog are stealing. The afternoon sun smolders in the drowsy sky. I have everything to make me glad I am alive."

"You're a poet," he said.

"Jack London said that. His vineyard is just across the valley here."

With June so relaxed, this was a good time to start back with his other questions. "I'm still curious about Odell and his new wife."

"Estelle. Nice girl. She's from another wine family in the valley. Her family's vines will now become a part of Naeper."

There sounded to be a bit of jealousy. "He seems to trust you so much," he said. "And you clearly know the operation here so well."

"Let me stop you there, mate. People always seem to wonder if Odell and I—let me put it this way. I love the guy as a human being. He makes me laugh. But we'd never work out. I'm too much like him. I want to be in control, and he lets me be so. Besides, I have a teenage daughter and want no more kids. He wants his own kids."

"I can see you're not shy," said Patton.

"No one's ever accused me of being shy," she said.

He noticed roses in full bloom at the bottom of each row. "That's a nice touch, roses," said Patton. "Adds to the beauty."

"Actually, they're like canaries in a coal mine, acting as a warning sign. If the roses get mildew, then it's time to spray the vines to keep away powdery mildew."

"With what?"

"Sulphur—it's allowed in organic farms—but we simply try to avoid mildew conditions, such as using low-drip irrigation, and we cut off flag shoots."

"Do vineyards have any kind of bug infestations?"

She looked at him curiously.

"I'm a home gardener, too," said Patton, not revealing what he really knew. "Aphids are always a big problem with me, so I use ladybugs."

"The grape leafhopper is one of our pests," said June, "as is the grape berry moth. This time of year, we plant certain flowering plants between the rows to help us out."

At Patton's feet lay a golf ball. He bent down, picked it up, and without thinking, threw it out along where Odell drove. The ball arced beautifully, going deep and plunging between rows.

"You have a good arm," said June.

"I played baseball in high school. In fact, I wanted to pursue a professional career in it, but I snapped a ligament behind my knee skiing—out went that career. What the heck. I found a better one."

"Detecting," she said as a statement.

He nodded, owning the word. "Yeah." A thought occurred to Patton. "Did Samantha want kids?"

"I know bugger all," she said. His frown must have made her add, "That's to say, I know nothing about that. You'll have to ask Odell."

"It's not important. I'm more curious why she had to leave so fast."

"We're curious, too."

Patton left shortly thereafter, but not before June insisted he take a bottle of their wine. They returned to her office where she looked over a small wine rack against her wall.

"You like white or red?" she asked.

"White."

"How about a Fume Blanc, then, mate?" She handed him a bottle that had a gold ribbon tied around it already.

"Thanks." He shook her hand.

As he left, he tried to picture Samantha in this place. She had had a good lifestyle in bloom. She would have been virtual royalty here. So what would make her leave? Another person in Sonoma? What would she suddenly not like about married life that she had to run away? Maybe she didn't want kids and he did? This was a leap, but if she'd been molested when she was younger—more than just a grope—it could be a reason not to have kids. Could Odell be that angry, though, to kill her?

As he walked past the receptionist in the lobby, she said, "Good night Mr. Burch." She was standing, collecting her purse. Her computer was off and the desk was now clear.

"Oh, thanks. Good night," he said. She walked out with him.

"Say," he asked her. "Might there be an inexpensive motel around here?"

"How inexpensive?" she asked.

"As cheap as they come."

She shook her head. "This is tourist country. But if you head toward Sonoma on Highway 12, the next town up is Boyes Hot Springs. That's where a lot of the laborers live. Cheap. There's a nice little motel called the Hot Springs Inn."

— ✣ —

Patton drove into Boyes Hot Springs and found the Hot Springs Inn right on Highway 12 just as promised, beyond a trailer park with small trees. The motel was small and pinkish with courtyard parking and the promise of HBO in each room. At the front counter, a young man gave him the rates—indeed inexpensive—and Patton took a room. After he hauled his bag into the room—clean with a queen-size bed and a round table with two chairs—he walked to Hermanos Tacos across the street. The small stucco-sided building had parking all around without a spot to be had, it appeared. He opened the screen door to find a simple restaurant with white square tables and wood chairs on a concrete floor—and every table full. However, no one was eating at the counter, which had high-backed stools. He sat there and ordered his usual Mexican fare: chicken enchilada, rice, beans, and a beer, Dos Equis.

As he ate, he heard the name "Naeper" and then an expletive. He turned, pretending to look outside for someone. Three men spoke Spanish in a serious tone. He didn't understand much, though the word "botellas" he recognized as bottles, having ordered a number of botellas of Dos Equis in his day. He also recognized the short man with slicked-back black hair and a graying goatee who was speaking earnestly now. He'd been in the bottling room. In response to something one of his comrades said, the man shook his head and said, "No way. Cuarenta mil bottellas solamente."

One of the other men said something in Spanish angrily, and the third man looked sad and resigned. Patton wondered if this was about employment, but he had no way of knowing. He wished he knew what they were saying. Every bit of information helped.

Patton turned back to his food, and about five minutes later, he noticed the man with the goatee walking down the hallway to the restroom. Patton decided to go there, too. When he stepped in, the man stood at one of two urinals, staring vacantly ahead. Patton decided to act a little drunk, and he stepped to the other urinal. He unzipped and let out a big sigh.

"Ah, a good feeling, eh?" said Patton. "They say we only rent beer."

"True." The man gave a quick glance. "Did I see you somewhere earlier today?" said the man in unaccented English. He'd probably grown up here.

"I was getting a tour of Naeper. You were in the bottling room, weren't you?"

"Yes."

"A hundred thousand cases, June said, for this year."

"No way," said the man, zipping up. "Usually wineries underreport their case counts—the snob factor, you know. I don't know why June told you more. We don't have that kind of volume—just over three thousand cases only this month. We'll be laid off in another week."

"Sorry to hear," said Patton.

"I work at other places, too," said the man, washing up. "Take care." And he left.

Interesting, thought Patton. Nothing said you had to give the public the real figures. This news had nothing to do with Samantha, yet he felt good in finding it out.

Patton finished up his meal, paid his bill, and returned to his room at the motel. His door was partially open. He paused. Was the maid there for some reason?

"Hello?" said Patton warily, pushing open the door.

"Hello" came a response, much the way Tess would say it.

Tess sat on the bed.

"Tess?" This felt surreal. She wore black jeans and a black T-shirt that said, "Welcome to Miami Beach." That was from a vacation they'd taken two years ago to go to her niece's wedding. Tess sat on the bed's edge, hands on her legs, straightfaced.

As stunned as he was, he felt a moment of weightlessness as he did at the top of a roller coaster. Here she was. If you wished for something hard enough, it could happen? "How did you get here?" he said.

"Flew. Rented a car."

"You know what I mean." He rushed to the closest window. "What about the FBI?" he said. "Are they going to swarm in on both of us?" No SWAT teams appeared in the bushes. A mangy-looking collie trotted past, gazed at Patton, apparently saw nothing of interest, and walked off.

"Brian helped me with the FBI."

"So you brought them to me!"

"I came alone. No one knows where I am."

"How'd you find me?"

"Brian said you were headed into Santa Rosa—and with client/attorney privilege, he didn't tell the FBI. He said I should find you."

"Santa Rosa's a big place—and we're in Boyes Hot Springs."

CHAPTER 15

"You told Brian Chatterley's real name, and I found the Malkeys from there. They told me about the Naeper Winery. By then it was after five, and I figured you wouldn't sleep in your van but find a motel. I looked for motels closest to Naeper, which brought me here to Boyes Hot Springs. There were a couple, and I found your van here."

"But why are you here?" He grinned, thinking he must have done something right, but he didn't know what. "Are we making up?"

"I don't know. That girl's death and the money laundering with Birnham—can't be coincidence, I thought."

He had to pause to process what she was saying. He remembered Brian saying she'd been going through Birnam's emails. "You found something on Birnam?"

"When Birnam took me out to lunch most recently, he ordered a good bottle of wine. I'd got to talking about the wine country tour you and I once took. He told me he loves going to vineyards—and that until recently he'd lived in Santa Rosa."

"Doesn't mean Samantha and Birnam are in any way connected."

"Actually, when I mentioned I was looking for a model to be a ladybug, he was the one to tell me about the modeling agency. He even suggested Chatterley."

Patton stared at her, shaking his head. "Why the hell didn't you tell me this earlier? This is a major connection."

"I didn't think of it. That agency lady, Joan Rivers, showed me a lot of photos when I flew in, and then I'd mentioned Chatterley, and I liked her shots. She seemed fine, wholesome yet sexy—not that I expected you to have an affair with her."

"And I didn't. So that's why you didn't tell me this important information?"

"I forgot. It wasn't on my mind. Sorry."

"So both people come from the same place—and Birnam knew her. I wonder if his scam and our hiring her had deeper connection."

"What do you mean?"

"Was his scam dependent on our hiring her?"

"I don't see how. He never asked about her, and I didn't mention it."

"This is the kind of thing the FBI should know about."

"Speaking of that, Brian arranged a phone conversation for me with an FBI agent. You were right about something you guessed earlier."

"What's that?"

"The money that was wired to us comes from the mob. I said the whole point of such a bank is to keep it private, so how did they know? He said they knew."

Patton nodded. It was nice to be right at something. He was also reminded why they made such good business partners—she was adept at following up details. "You're saying Italians are involved?" he asked.

"I don't know their ethnic background."

"But you're saying the money comes from the mob, and if the mob's involved, they might be here in Sonoma."

"Maybe."

"And because Samantha was here and Birnam knew her, maybe the mob had something to do with Samantha's death?"

"The FBI agent didn't say that. He hardly told me anything—but the two things could be connected, seems to me."

"If you found me this easily, might the FBI?"

"They don't know you like I do."

"So I'm not dreaming you," he said. He took one of her hands.

She pulled her hand away. "Listen, I'm not saying our problems are over. Yesterday you said we needed to work together, and now I'm convinced of that. Two heads are better than one, particularly since the police and FBI don't seem to be helping us."

He found himself smiling. She didn't look away. For a moment at least, with her in front of him, Patton sensed all was right in the world.

She was about to say something, and he put one finger gently on her lips.

"Don't say anything just yet," he said. "I need this."

* * *

Tess hadn't eaten anything since breakfast, so he took her to Hermanos Tacos where he drank another Dos Equis, and she ate a chicken tostada. He caught up with more of the details of her flying up and finding him. She thought the Malkeys were nice, but they'd made her very uncomfortable.

"They thought I knew their daughter and were showing me pictures of her. She was very pretty."

He gritted his teeth. "She was." This wasn't the conversation he wanted to be having.

"I can see why you were attracted."

"Please, Tess. If attraction is a crime, okay I'm guilty. But she was sick that night, she died, and I'm starting to wonder if you're using this as a way to get back at me for other things."

"Such as what?"

"I don't know. She is not 'the other woman.'"

"What if she hadn't gotten sick? What would have happened then in your room?"

"Maybe we shouldn't talk about her."

"That's what I thought." She looked like a winning prosecutor.

He leaned closer. "What if Birnam was younger and handsomer? He had all that money. Would you have an affair with him?"

"That's stupid."

"How's it any more stupid than your hypothetical? You want to argue over a hypothetical?" This wasn't the relaxed, getting-to-be-friends-with-you-again dining he'd hoped for.

"How do you fix an event that can't be erased?"

"That's what I'm asking myself, too," said Patton. "How do other people get through terrible things? Like people who lose children or lose a leg in Iraq."

"It's not comparable, Patton. How can you measure one bad thing against another?"

"I'm not trying to measure. I'm trying to figure out how to get through this. In the meantime, someone murdered this young woman, and if it's the mob, I mean, what kind of resources do we have? How do we find them?"

"A better question might be how won't they find us and how can we stay alive? You've been poking around here asking questions. Someone may be taking notice already. We don't want to get killed."

"I haven't been worried."

"I figured. I'm glad I'm here to keep you alive."

"That's why you're here?"

She looked at him more softly now. She nodded.

— ❦ —

When they returned to the room, he said, "This place comes with HBO. Should we see what's on? Or would you like to go into Sonoma, walk around the square together?"

"I'm beat. Staying in sounds good." She looked at the bed, then the TV. "Maybe I should call for a cot. Would you mind sleeping on a cot?"

He didn't answer instantly. Was this how it was going to be—he had to pay some kind of penance? "How about if we sleep in the same bed and not touch? We're kind of used to that anyway, aren't we? We can just pretend it's like the usual."

She sighed and took a side of the bed, propping up the pillows against the headboard. "Turn on HBO. Let's see what's there."

Patton clicked on the TV. Onscreen, a handsome young man looked at a young woman in a T-shirt as she approached her car. The man smiled deviously, and fangs appeared. It was some sort of vampire thing.

"Is this okay?" Patton asked.

"Fine," she said.

He plopped down on his side of the bed.

The vampire called out, "Hey," and the young woman waved him over and said, "Would you like to come over for a Dos Equis?"

"She likes your beer," said Tess. "Wonder what that means?"

In short order it meant the young woman was naked, and so was the vampire, and they were having passionate sex. Is that what modern vampires had to do these days before the red stuff flowed? Patton felt uncomfortable. The young naked couple only showed what he and Tess, husband and wife, could not do.

"Mind if I look for something else?" he said.

"I'm going to wash up." Tess stood, grabbed her overnight bag, and rolled it into the bathroom. She didn't look at him, even as she closed the door. This evening was going to require something else, Patton could see.

He changed the channel, and up came the sitcom Two and a Half Men. Charlie Sheen was in bed with a woman who truly seemed to adore him and probably would have sex with him shortly. He switched channels, and up came a young red-headed woman staring happily at a young man without fangs, just an am-I-lucky smile. "I'd be happy to see you again," said the woman. "If you stop seeing Rachel."

He turned off the TV. It wasn't his friend. He wanted things to go well with Tess, but now some subtle shift had occurred. He felt as helpless as a dog in a pound.

Fifteen minutes later, Tess emerged, and he hadn't moved. She wore the key lime pajamas that he'd bought her about four years earlier. As she walked he noticed the sway of her breasts under the slippery silk. Was she smiling?

"Nothing on TV?" she said.

"Not really."

She gently sat next to him. And moved closer. The scent of roses and a hint of vanilla became apparent.

"A new perfume?" he said.

"I kind of liked that vampire thing. You didn't?"

"If you want to watch it…"

He left it at that.

She looked at him. Definitely she had a slight smile. Her hair was swept back, which made him notice new stud earrings with blue and clear stones with many facets—elegant.

"Have I seen your earrings before?" he said.

"What if I said you bought them for me?"

"Did I?"

"Yes, for my birthday five years ago."

"I remember shopping in Pasadena… Diamonds and something."

"Yes, diamonds and my birthstone, blue topaz."

"They're gorgeous."

"I've always loved them."

"Thanks."

Her hints were there, but were they hints? He hated this about himself. He didn't want to make the wrong move. He wanted so much to kiss her and say he wanted to make love to her.

He laughed.

"What?" she said.

"When we first got married, I thought marriage would make things easier when it came to… you know."

"What?" she said again, and he knew that she knew, and he leaned in, gently took her head, and touched her lips with his. They kissed like teenagers for a few minutes, her hands on his shoulders, his hands on her arms. Her mouth tasted not the usual mint toothpaste, but something new. Cherry. She pushed against him, kissed him with urgency. That only made him want her more, but one thing he learned, probably took him fifteen years, was don't rush things.

He slipped his hands under her top in the back so he could feel her skin, which felt smooth, welcoming. His fingers found her shoulder blades, which he'd always thought sexy. She pulled up his shirt in the back then yanked his shirt off him.

He pulled off her top.

She smelled great, and as she embraced him, her breasts pressed against his chest like two warm palms.

They didn't rush things, though he surprised himself when he finally entered her and she felt so incredibly soft and slippery. They never used condoms because the pill worked so well. He worried he might come too early, but he just couldn't stop. She seemed to sense this because she stopped all motion.

"Hold on," she whispered and disengaged.

"I'm sorry. It just feels good."

"It's okay," she said. "Let's just pause here a little bit." She gave little butterfly kisses to his chest. He forced himself to think about other things, and he thought about the van. He should get new tires for the van. They were getting a little bald.

In moments, though, he left his tires behind and was back to simply sensing Tess. He loved how delicate her hands were. They fit his so well. She gently turned him to his back and straddled him, guiding him in. He couldn't help but think of his mother's advice from his grandmother—to sometimes be on the bottom, and he laughed.

"What?" said Tess.

"Being on the bottom isn't bad."

In a few more minutes, they were back to where they had been, but this time she was the one moving hard, and he let her, willing himself to breathe steadily and be tantric, staying hard. After several more minutes, they tried another position, and then another. Years ago when she first suggested doggie style, he didn't think he could do it because, well, it seemed wrong. He didn't know why, but it had seemed so male fantasy. She had said it felt good, and now he was reminded how it felt good for him, too. It was their own personal dance.

Afterwards, they cuddled under the sheet, her head on his chest.

He thought of his friend Barry from high school and laughed.

"What's so funny?" she asked.

"I don't know why I thought of it now, but my friend Barry Ekstrand in high school brought in the Bible one day and had us read the Song of Songs. He said there was great sex in there, which was long before any of us had sex. He read where a woman says, 'I sat down under his shadow with great delight, and his fruit was sweet to my taste.' I remember that line." He laughed, and she smiled.

"Is the real thing better?"

"Much."

Snuggled up against each other, they watched TV for a while, the end of a stand-up comic's routine on HBO. The guy was a short Mexican man he'd never seen. When a documentary came on, he clicked it off. She used the bathroom, and when she returned, she looked serious, lost in thought.

"What're you thinking?" he asked.

"Nothing," she said and closed her eyes.

He said, "I don't believe it."

CHAPTER 15

And she said to the room, "I can't help it. I wonder if I'm better than her. Samantha."

"Tess. Believe me, I wouldn't know. You're beautiful and sexy and there's no point on focusing on anything else."

"I'm not sure that'll ever go away."

He didn't know what to say to that. He turned out the lights and in the dark, kissed her good night. They turned on their sides, away from each other.

CHAPTER 16 (DAY 8)

Tess had refused a breakfast burrito at Hermanos Tacos, and she'd said the guy at the motel's front desk recommended the Big Three Bistro at the Sonoma Mission Inn and Spa—a short walk from their motel. Patton knew that anyplace with the word "spa" in it would be expensive, but he had to admit this was the perfect place for their first breakfast—white table cloths and French windows that opened out onto rose bushes in full bloom. Tess looked gorgeous in a light-blue sweater.

"Is your hollandaise sauce for the Benedict lemony?" Tess asked the waiter in a vest and trim beard. "My husband likes a real lemony sauce," she said, pointing to Patton.

"Wonderfully tart," said their waiter, "but I can bring you a few lemon wedges, too."

"Thanks. And she likes a slice of avocado with her Benedict, if that's possible—unless you're going for the pancakes," he said to Tess.

"I do like avocado," she said.

"Of course," said the waiter, who bowed slightly as he left.

Tess buttered a slice of sourdough bread from the basket. "Listen," she said, "I realize that there must be things I've done, too, to push us apart. I haven't been a good wife, I suppose."

"What do you mean?" He'd never seen her admit to a weakness before.

"Kids, for one—I've avoided parenthood. And look at our lives. Besides the business and traveling, what do we have in common anymore? What things do we do together?"

It sounded to him as if she were making a case for divorce. "No," he said, perhaps too quickly or loudly. "We have lots in common. We like skiing, reading. We like a clean house, we—"

"Maybe we're over."

"And maybe we're not," he said.

"You know what I feel like?" she said. "Like a politician's wife who has to stand in front of reporters and smile while her philandering husband says he's sorry to the world. I always thought I knew you, could rely on you, and then this happened."

"It wasn't anything I'd planned. I'm sorry. It's like trying to explain why there was an earthquake."

"There was? Where?"

"I'm just giving it as an example. There wasn't one."

"That's not a good example. Didn't you even consider me when…."

She paused, and he knew what she was trying to say and immediately said, "No. All I can say is the human mind…. It permits people to do things that are rationally wrong."

"I don't get it." Her eyes watered up, pooling quickly, and two tears dropped. She turned away from him.

"I've always tried to do the right thing. I don't completely understand what happened." Seeing her silently crying and wiping her eyes, though, made him remember a morning many months before Las Vegas. It was in November just after daylight savings time had ended, and he'd awakened and felt completely awake. He could see his hand in dim light, and he'd wondered if there was a full moon or was the dawn coming?

The digital bedside clock showed that it was just before 5:30. He sat up and strode to the door of his and Tess's bedroom porch, which overlooked their hill. Street lights still twinkled in the valley, but there was no moon in the sky. Morning was coming. He thought about getting back in bed, but as he stared at Tess, curled in sleep with one of the cats cocooned at her side, he realized she was complete. She didn't really need him, did she? They hadn't made love in months—hadn't been particularly affectionate even for a while—and he'd felt something then. Very empty. He looked around the room in the gray light. Everything was mere shapes. These shapes would last longer than he would. Would he be in that same room in thirty years? Would his bad knee have him hobbling around. Maybe he'd barely be able to walk in the future. He remembered thinking he just wanted somebody to love.

Rather than dwell on it then, he'd found his briefcase and slipped upstairs to work. Now, here before Tess who was still turned away, he realized he'd felt what she was feeling. It was wanting to connect and being unable to—but they had last night.

He touched her arm. "Maybe this unerasable thing, as you call it," he said, "will fade. Maybe there's a way back."

She stiffened, appearing more businesslike. She wiped the tears as if it'd been silly. She was doing the same thing he'd done by going to the kitchen table. Work was a good distraction. "How about if we focus on what we're here for?" she said.

"Sure," he said, wondering what else he could say.

"And if we get through our bigger problems, maybe we can go to a marriage counselor together—or each to a psychologist."

"I've never believed in shrinks," he said, "but if it'll help you, hey, show me the way."

"Like you don't need a shrink? If you can't explain what you did, don't you think you need to find out how it happened? When a jet falls out of the sky, the black box is examined, no? We need to look at your black box."

"And yours, too," he said, glaring right at her. He realized she could make him mad in an instant. He didn't want that.

She sighed. "Okay, we'll look through my wreckage, too." She reached out and took his hand. "Okay?"

He agreed. They held hands for a few minutes, saying nothing more.

"So you mentioned last night we needed to research the mob up here. What do you mean and how? We don't just Google 'mob in wine country,' I assume.

"No, but we can go to the website of a newspaper in the wine country," he said. "But my laptop's out of commission." It occurred to him that he didn't remember bringing his computer into the motel room. Was it still in the van? He remembered carrying his case into the winery, but not back out. Shit. He'd left it at Naeper.

"It's out?"

"Someone tripped on my cord at Starbucks, and the screen broke. I'll get it fixed."

"Didn't I tell you to be careful the last time at Starbucks?"

"Yes, but you weren't here this time, and I didn't anticipate. I'm sorry. I also forgot the computer at the winery."

"Patton," she said in the way only she could say it, which, to be frank, was not something he wanted to be reminded of. "Sometimes I wonder about you," she continued. "I swear, you're just like…" She didn't finish the sentence.

A kid, she surely meant to say. The fact she didn't say it was important.

CHAPTER 16

She was trying to make things work, too. He smiled. "I'll call them later. We'll have to stop by the winery sometime, and we'll also need to take your rented car back. The bigger point is that we can't research on my computer because it's broken."

"Didn't I say we should have one of the new cell phones with the Internet on it?"

"Those are for kids."

"I noticed a sign for a business center in this hotel," she said. "It said guests could print out their boarding passes."

"You're thinking we could use one of their computers?" he said.

She nodded, seemingly proud of herself. "If we're friendly enough to our waiter, we can probably use it. So what do you want to look up?"

"Because mobsters don't call attention to their deeds or identity in the media, let's see if there're any stories about murders or disappearances up here. Maybe they'd be mob-related."

She looked at him, nodding.

After breakfast, the waiter said of course they could use the business center. They found the small room had a few desks and computers. No one else was there, so they pulled an extra chair to the first desk. Patton typed while Tess watched. He found the website for the Santa Rosa Press Democrat.

"This is the local paper," he said.

She nodded.

In the website's search window, he typed the word "murder." Up came several stories, all local but over several months. There were a few about a husband or wife murdering a spouse. He shook his head at that. People could get so mad, they just didn't think—a terrible flaw in the human condition.

Tess pointed to the headline, "Mysterious Playground Burial Still Unsolved." She said, "Click on this one."

He did, and they read about a winery worker's body discovered in the sand of a children's playground in a public park. After two months, police still didn't know who killed him or why. A child, of course, first found a hand, and police were asking why would someone dig a shallow grave in a playground? "It was probably a fast and quick place to dig," speculated a detective. Patton wondered why say "fast and quick?" They were the same thing.

He returned to the headlines, scrolled down, and Tess pointed to another headline, "DNA of Bones Still Doesn't Explain Anything." They read another story of an unexplained murder. A human skeleton was found attached to an anchor in Lake Ralphine in Howarth Park. Police speculated the body could have been down there a year.

"That's interesting," said Patton.

"How so?" she asked.

"Two unsolved murders in a year, and both look to be disposals of bodies." He noted the writer of the article: Melodia Perkins. He returned to the first article and looked to see who wrote it: also Melodia Perkins.

"We should call her," Patton said. "She seems to be on the police beat. Maybe she'd know if there's any mob activity around here."

"We didn't find any articles on mob activity."

"She'll have a good overview of crime up here—and may know about the mob."

"What about Birnam?" Tess asked.

He typed in Birnam's name into the search box, but nothing came up in the newspaper about him.

Patton found the number for the Press Democrat. He pulled out his cell phone. "Do you think it's okay to use this now?" he asked Tess.

"We're okay with the FBI. They're no longer looking for us."

"Not for me, either?"

"I told you Brian fixed it for now."

He wanted to know more, but he called the newspaper and asked for Melodia Perkins. The phone rang twice before a woman answered, "Perkins."

"Ms. Perkins, my name is Patton Burch. I happen to be up in the area and—

"I'm on deadline. Can we talk later?" she said.

"Have a moment? This is important—about the mysterious disappearance of a woman named—"

"Is this a missing persons thing?"

"Murder," he said.

There was a slight pause. "Now you have my attention," she said. "Go on."

"A woman named Samantha Malkey went missing from the area about a year ago."

"I don't remember hearing about that."

"She assured her family she was fine, but she was hiding out."

"From what?"

"That's why I'm involved. I'm trying to figure that out. She lived in Las Vegas under a false identity, and whatever reason she fled from here may have caught up with her—and killed her. "

Chapter 16

"Are you a police detective?"

"No. Private," he said, not wanting to lose her attention.

"Tell me more about Samantha Malkey."

He explained more and told her about Birnam, adding, "Now we're trying to do research about the mob up here. You seem like someone who might know. We happened to come across a couple of articles that you wrote about unsolved murders."

"Who's we?"

"My colleague Tess, who's also my wife." He looked at Tess as he said the last part. She gave a short nod.

"I'd like to meet you, if that's possible," Ms. Perkins said. "Can you come to my office on Mendocino Avenue in Santa Rosa? The Press Democrat is near the 101, not far from College Avenue."

"I'll Google it. We can meet soon, if you like. We're in Boyes Hot Springs."

"That'll take you thirty to forty minutes—perfect. I'll be done with my story by then."

Patton and Tess drove there separately. After their meeting with the reporter, they'd return Tess's rental car. On the way, he called the Naeper winery and, pushing O for Operator, heard a monotone voice say, "Naeper Winery. May I help you?" He recognized the woman at the front desk, and he reminded her of who he was and how he'd left his computer in the library. She said she'd bring it to the front desk for him.

"How late can I come?" he asked. "I'm trying to fit in a lot today."

"If you can't make it by three, come this evening after six. We have a wedding reception, so use the valet, and someone will be at the front desk—maybe me."

"Many thanks."

The Press Democrat building was a three-story modern-looking box across the street from the Super Buffet and Armed Forces Career Center.

Melodia Perkins's office was on the third floor. She had what looked like one of the few cherished window offices at the edge of the pressroom. A young African-American woman in her late twenties, with straight black hair curled at the bottom, she spoke into her desk phone as they approached the open door of her office. She leaned into the phone, unaware of them, and said, "Yes, it's done…. Of course I do, why do you treat me like that?… Fuck it." She slammed her phone down, and only then noticed them at the doorway. She looked embarrassed at first but quickly straightened. Patton figured it must have been a personal call, perhaps a boyfriend.

"So you're Patton Burch?"

"Yes." They shook hands, and she looked him right in the eyes as if trying to find something. "And this is my wife, Tess."

Ms. Perkins didn't smile, but shook her hand. "Please sit," she said, pointing to two chairs against the wall. Before she sat, she said, "May I see your private detective's license, Mr. Burch? I always ask this of police and private detectives I don't know."

"Oh." He considered reaching for his wallet and then being surprised, but even the thought seemed lame. He just said, "I don't have it with me."

"That's because you don't have one. I'm a reporter with access to a lot of databases. Did I sound young and dumb on the phone? You're wanted for murder."

"I am," he said.

"And you're involved, too?" she asked Tess.

"Not in a murder."

"You know I can bring the police with just one phone call."

"We need your help, and you'll get a hell of a story," said Patton.

"Good. That's what I'm hoping for. I need a big story."

"Melodia," came a loud voice, and a tall black man in a white short-sleeved shirt and blue tie appeared at the door. When he saw Patton and Tess, his demeanor changed. "Oh. Sorry. I didn't know Melodia had…" He looked at Melodia and said, one word: "Sorry." His apology wasn't about barging in, Patton sensed. It was more intimate.

"And I'm sorry I won't be able to make lunch today," she told him. "I've got a new story developing."

The man looked more closely at Patton and Tess, nodded, said, "Okay." He didn't look pleased. He also wore a wedding ring. If the man were having an affair with Melodia, Patton hoped it wouldn't get in the way of what he and Tess needed. The man turned and left.

"We're trying to connect Samantha Malkey's death in Las Vegas to here," said Patton. "So do you know if there's organized crime up here?"

Melodia stared out the doorway a moment, still apparently caught up with the man with the blue tie. She looked at Patton. "Nothing provable," she said. "This valley certainly isn't a crime hub of any sort."

"What about those two unsolved murders?" said Tess.

"According to my boss," she said, thumbing to no one at the door, "those murders are not a sign of anything."

"That was your boss?" Tess said.

Melodia nodded. "I also researched the man you mentioned, Anton Birnam. Nothing in the news, but he's an accountant with a private accounting firm in Santa Rosa."

"Any big names for clients?" said Patton.

"No telling. It's a private firm."

Patton shook his head. They were getting nowhere fast.

"What interested me about your call," said Melodia, "is that I do think there's organized crime up here. Ernie Josephs, who owns Wolfhound Vineyards, has reputed ties to the mob in New York. The winery worker found buried in the playground worked next door to Wolfhound. Here's a picture of Josephs."

She pushed across a color 4x6 that showed a square-jawed man with thick hair and a gray mustache that reminded him not of an Italian mobster but of actor Tom Selleck—someone who could be both friendly and ruthless. His pale blue eyes appeared as if they'd seen a hundred murders, but his smile made it seem that he only saw ice cream trucks.

"I never heard of Wolfhound wine," said Tess.

"And why wasn't Josephs mentioned in the article?" said Patton.

"We can't accuse him of anything. And Josephs is a generous man in the Valley."

"I haven't heard of Wolfhound, either," said Patton.

"There is no Wolfhound label. He has fifty prime acres—nearly the first place out of Santa Rosa as you head toward Sonoma. He sells the grapes to a handful of wineries. Many of the smaller wineries like Wellington need to buy grapes to have enough production."

Patton leaned forward. This is what he needed. "Tell us more."

"Officially, he's a businessman from New York who came here to retire in a nice little vineyard. Everyone wants to be in the wine business."

"Maybe some guys can't help themselves—and then you get two odd unsolved murders," Patton said. "So how can we interview this guy?"

"No way," said Tess. "If he's organized crime and he's involved, we could be at the end of an anchor in the local lake, too."

"That's sort of why my boss hasn't wanted me to interview him. I have another idea," said Melodia. "I heard Josephs' vineyard manager, Paul Cromwell, has left Wolfhound for a better job at a bigger vineyard, Russian Cascade."

"In Russia?" said Tess.

"The Russian River is near here. Paul is well known in the area—a down-to-earth guy. I've been wanting to interview him about something else in hopes he'd say something about Josephs—if I were subtle enough."

"How would you do that?" Tess asked.

"Maybe tell him I'm doing a story about viticulturists and vineyard managers."

"What's the difference?" Patton asked.

"A lot. And in talking about what he did at Wolfhound, I'd slip in questions about Josephs. I bet Cromwell has seen things."

"If you're a crime beat reporter, wouldn't he suspect something?"

"It's not like I'm a household name."

"Can you do it soon?"

"It takes time and footwork," she said.

"I don't have time," Patton said. "I have to give myself up soon to the Vegas police."

Her phone buzzed. She looked at the readout and sighed. "That's the best I can do," she told Patton. "You have to be patient." They quickly shook her hand while she picked up the phone with the other.

As they walked out, Patton turned to Tess. "I don't think she'll do it right away."

"You heard her. She'll do it."

"We have to do something sooner."

As they neared the stairs, Patton saw that the last office was occupied by Melodia's boss. He looked contrite as he spoke into his phone. The name "Stanley Barnes" was etched on his door glass.

"We can interview Cromwell," Patton said to Tess in the stairwell, "if we pretend we work here."

"We're going to lie?"

"If it'll help us." Patton stopped to look at Tess directly. "We have to act quickly and play roles. We have to be different people. She told us all we needed to know—who Cromwell is and where to find him. Russian Cascade. If we can more directly connect mob money and Samantha leaving this area, maybe I can get out of my mess."

"And what if Samantha left for another reason? Maybe there are coincidences here," she said. "I feel uneasy about this."

"And I'll feel worse in prison."

— ✿ —

"Mr. Cromwell," said Patton into his cell phone out on the sidewalk. Tess stood next to him, looking doubtful. "This is Stanley Barnes with the Press Democrat—you read the paper, right?"

"I've been mentioned in it a few times over the years," said Cromwell. "Is this for a subscription?"

Patton held a folded section of a newspaper before him, open to the Lifestyle section. "No. I'm one of the head editors here, and I'm working with a new reporter who did a little research and found you're working at this new vineyard."

"Yes."

"While we've often had stories on the wine industry, I realized we've never really done a story on vineyard management versus viticulturists. We'd love to interview you—maybe even turn it into a full-fledged story on you."

"Really? Just on me?"

"Absolutely. Is it possible to meet with you for an interview?"

"Today or when?"

"The sooner the better."

"I have a thick schedule this afternoon, ending with a meeting in Kenwood at four."

Kenwood sounded familiar to Patton, but he couldn't ask where it was, blowing his cover as a local. "Could we meet in Kenwood after your meeting?" said Patton.

"Sure, around five? Say at Café Porta Via?"

"Sounds great," said Patton. They had a few hours to find it. "How will I know you?"

"I'm wearing a black Valley of the Moon t-shirt today."

"Wonderful, and I'm wearing a yellow shirt." Patton hung up with a smile for Tess. "We have an appointment, late afternoon."

They returned Tess's rental car just past noon and took the clerk's advice for a good place for lunch: Hank's Creekside on Fourth. They burned a few more hours at the Jack London State Historic Park in Glen Ellen, which was 40 acres of writer London's original 1413-acre Beauty Ranch. On the way there on Highway 12, they came across Café Porta Via on the right side of the road.

At four-thirty, they left for Café Porta Via, mere minutes away. The restaurant seemed more like a deli. The place was dominated by a large refrigerated display case, and the place was two-thirds full—surprising, considering it wasn't dinnertime yet. Patton headed toward two empty tables toward the back. Next to one of them, a man with comb-over blond hair in his late thirties leaned close to a young woman in her early-twenties and said perhaps too enthusiastically, "I'm glad you finally graduated!" His neck and shoulders were wide, and with his sports jacket, he appeared to be a professor who'd dumped his wife for a Corvette and a Nautilus membership. When the young woman smiled, her braces showed.

Patton chose the table farthest from them. He ordered two cappuccinos.

Before their order came, Patton spotted a tall, thin man, perhaps early fifties, in John Lennon glasses and a black t-shirt with the words "Valley of the Moon" on the front. Patton rose and waved, and the man nodded, smiled, and headed over. He looked like a friendly guy with tan, leathery skin.

"I'm Stanley," Patton said, "and this is Tess." They shook hands and sat.

Patton had realized on the way there that reporters probably recorded things, but he didn't have a recorder. He pulled out his cell phone now and said, "Mind if I record our interview—with my phone? Cell phones do everything these days."

Paul laughed. "Yeah, I'm waiting for the one that does my laundry. Recording this is fine." Patton pretended to push a button on the side of his phone. He knew other phones had this feature, but his didn't.

He also hadn't been able to research anything about Mr. Cromwell or what he did, but this being an interview, he'd let the man explain. "So let's start with the difference between vineyard manager and viticulturist. How do you define each?"

Cromwell leaned closer to the cell phone as if to be sure every word was caught. "A viticulturist is someone concerned with the science or art of cultivating the soil—for grape vines specifically. A vineyard manager manages farming operations from pruning and irrigation to the harvest of grapes. He's a big picture kind of guy. He—or she—hires and fires people and makes sure things are done on time. A manager surely knows a lot about plant botany but might also hire a freelancer with a degree in viticulture or enology." Cromwell looked pleased at his answer.

"And where might our readers get one of these degrees?" said Tess, writing in her small notebook, which she always carried in her purse for ideas about the business. She looked like a reporter, too.

"The local colleges here have programs in both. There's management and enology courses at Santa Rosa Junior College, where I sometimes teach. Cal State Sonoma has a whole business degree in the wine business."

Patton nodded. "I understand you worked at Wolfhound Vineyard for a number of years."

"Yes, the last four."

"Was Ernie Josephs a good person to work for?"

"Oh, yeah—a great guy."

"I heard he'd been in the mob." Patton said it with a smile to make it seem not like a big deal.

"I heard those rumors. All I know is he loves his grapes, and whatever life he had before, he's retired from it." Paul smiled, too. It came across as if he'd said it many times.

"Was Josephs a hands-on kind of person, or did he let you run things as you saw fit?"

"When we started, he didn't know a lot about the wine business other than he loved drinking the stuff. I've taught him a lot, and he let me run things. He now has some of the best grapes in the business."

"You probably heard about a couple of unsolved murders in Sonoma," said Tess. "One body found in a playground, the other at the end of an anchor in a lake—did you ever wonder if Ernie Josephs was connected to those?"

Patton winced—too direct a question for right now. Cromwell frowned, then looked from Tess to Patton. "What's going on here? I thought this was an article on vineyard management. Is this just some trick?"

"It's about vineyard management," Patton said instantly. "Tess is new at this. The bodies came up on some background research on Mr. Josephs is all."

"I've never heard him linked to those, and I never—" Paul Cromwell stood. "That's enough. I don't want any article on me or about Mr. Josephs."

"I can promise you—"

But Cromwell had his hand up.

Patton opened the manila folder that he brought in with him. "Let me ask you one more question, Mr. Cromwell, and I won't run a story on you if you don't want." He put his phone away as if to emphasize that this was off the record, then pulled out his photo of Samantha. "Have you ever seen her before?"

Cromwell lifted the photo and with barely a glance said, "Samantha Malkey. What about her?"

"How do you know her?"

"She worked at the Naeper Winery. She was our point person until June LeCompte took over."

"What do you mean point person?" Tess asked.

"Wolfhound sells grapes to Naeper. Samantha was our liaison for a while."

Tess looked wide-eyed at Patton, and he felt as she looked. This was big news—a connection.

Patton looked at Cromwell. "Samantha was found murdered in Las Vegas."

Cromwell looked startled. "Murdered?" He sat again, as if trying to understand it. "You think Ernie Josephs had something to do with that? That's why we're meeting?" He shook his head. "I don't believe for a second that Ernie's involved. He adored Samantha like a daughter—both he and his wife. In fact, for the longest time they tried setting me up with her after my divorce. Then we found out she was secretly Odell's girl."

"Secretly?" said Tess.

"I don't know why it was a secret. Maybe he thought we wouldn't take Samantha as seriously in the business. Naeper is Wolfhound's biggest client."

"Biggest?" That meant Odell and Josephs were very important to each other. "And have you heard the name Anton Birnam?" Patton asked.

"He's Wolfhound's accountant. Ernie was a bit upset with the guy recently, but I don't know why. What's Birnam have to do with anything?" Cromwell still looked shocked. The fact that he had slipped this information showed Patton how surprised Cromwell was.

"Birnam was in Las Vegas laundering money," said Tess.

Again Cromwell frowned. "Now why is it I'm hearing this stuff from reporters and not, say, a police detective?"

"The police aren't looking as closely as we are. And until now, we didn't have a connection between the wine country and Las Vegas. Now we do."

"Hey—and I'm serious. You didn't hear any of this from me."

"Strictly anonymous," said Patton.

"Josephs was always top-notch with me.... I just don't want to be connected, you follow me?"

"Yes," said Patton, shaking his hand.

He then left. Two tables over, the man with the comb-over hair said, "Hilary for president, no way! For one, she doesn't understand trickle-down economics."

Tess leaned over and kissed Patton on the cheek.

"What's that for?" he asked.

She pulled out her cell phone from her purse. "Because we now have the connection to Las Vegas. We have enough to let the experts take over."

"You mean the FBI?"

"Yeah—Brian, actually. He'll know what to do with the FBI." She flipped open her phone and looked through her list of names.

"Wait a second," he said. "Let's talk this out first. Maybe we should do a few more things."

She paused. "Such as what?"

"Let's talk this through. All the elements are there that Ernie Josephs had Samantha killed. Maybe she learned something and got out of here fast. He's mob and from New York, after all."

"And what could Samantha have learned to make her leave here?"

"About one or both of the murders here in the Valley."

"That may be a stretch. We don't have enough to know that."

"But can't you taste it? It just seems logical."

"It could be hundreds of things. Plus, if they found her in Vegas and wanted to stop her from testifying, why didn't they just shoot her and bury her in the desert?"

Patton tapped his chin. "I see what you're saying—that Samantha's killing was extremely personal. The killer knew about her asthma, and she wasn't just buried in the desert. I can't help but wonder if Josephs had an affair with her. Powerful men see beautiful women as a force to conquer, to own."

"Why would Samantha have an affair? She was engaged to Odell."

Patton couldn't help but nod. Tess was a wonderful foil. He said, "She kept their engagement secret so that she'd be seen as a professional. I'm thinking she went along with an affair to either get or keep Joseph's business."

"From what you said, though, she was well-grounded. She didn't use her beauty for that."

"Yes, and I could see how such intimacy would probably weigh on her—that and Josephs' dark secrets, she had to leave. She was way over her head."

"That still doesn't answer how you got involved and blamed for it."

"It was my bad luck."

"What about Odell?" she asked.

"He's just a schmuck whose heart was broken. If Josephs is his biggest supplier of grapes, Odell couldn't actually do anything even if he suspected."

"We have to bring in the FBI now."

"We don't have enough—it's all wild speculation. If it's coming from me, they'll think I'm making it up to get out of being the prime suspect in Samantha's death."

"What choice do we have?" said Tess.

"Josephs' weak link has to be Anton Birnam—who managed to find you."

"He needed to launder his money, as you said earlier. He clearly knew enough venture capitalists to get the word out."

Patton grabbed some of the extra silverware on the table: two forks, a knife, and a spoon. "Let's say these two forks are Josephs and Birnam." Holding one in each hand, he walked them toward each other like puppets.

"Hey, Birnam, how're my investments?" Patton said, moving one fork.

"Just fine," Patton said, moving the other fork, the Birnam fork.

Patton looked at Tess. "And then you came along." Dropping one fork, he grabbed the spoon and marched it toward Birnam fork. "Hey, Birnam. Want to invest in my company?"

"Sure, here," said the Birnam fork.

At this point, Patton put both forks in one hand and picked up the knife with the other. "Hello, gentlemen, I'm Samantha. I'm here to buy some of your grapes."

"Hubba Hubba." Both forks moved toward the knife.

"See," said Patton.

"That's it? That doesn't explain why Samantha was murdered."

"My point exactly. We've got to talk with Josephs."

Patton dropped the spoon and brought back the Josephs fork. "Hey, some of my money is missing. What can you tell me about it, Birnam?"

"I don't know." Patton smiled at Tess.

"Are the unsolved murders out?" said Tess, standing. "Let me think. I have to pee."

"Josephs did something. I know it. Cromwell said Josephs had been upset with the accountant. Birnam's hiding. If we called Josephs about Birnam, he might want to see us, and we'd know we're probably right. Maybe then we call the FBI. They can solve how Samantha fit in."

"If Josephs is as deadly as we think he is, he may deal with us before the FBI gets here," Tess said, doing a pee-pee dance.

"It's just a call is all I'm proposing. He doesn't have triangulation on us or anything."

"No way. It's far too dangerous, and I have to use the restroom," she said, rushing off. "Just hold on as I think this through more. Play with the silverware some more."

"I'm dyin' here. The Vegas police want to throw away the key on me. We need more."

But she was off. At least he had her interest.

The young woman two tables over told the man with the comb-over, "I think I want to try working in the fields, see what the grape pickers have to go through."

"But you have a degree," the man said, astonished.

"That and five bucks will get me a coffee here," she said.

"You're such a good artist, though. In fact, I want to show you the etchings I just bought."

Not the etchings, Patton thought. Maybe she was too young to realize that man was a boor trying to seduce her. Had he been her professor?

Patton considered what Tess would say about Josephs when she returned. She'd be conservative. She wouldn't let him call. Sometimes things were a power play with her. Nothing said she had to know.

With his cell phone, he got the number for Wolfhound Vineyards and called it. A message said it was after hours, but he pressed "O" for Operator, and a man with a baritone voice said, "Got something more?"

"I'm looking for Mr. Josephs," said Patton.

"Oh, I thought— This is Mr. Josephs. Who's this?"

"You don't know me, but my wife and I know of a scam by a man you know, Anton Birnam, in a money laundering thing. We were burned by him, too."

There was a long pause. "Who is this?"

"I don't know if I should say."

"The reporters at Porta Via?"

Patton's heart thumped. "Reporters?"

"My friend Cromwell just told me about Samantha. He knew how much my wife and I adored her."

Enough to have an affair? he wanted to say. He had to play cool while he quickly walked toward the bathroom for Tess. "I know where Anton Birnam is."

"You don't know shit, and how'd you know Samantha? Or maybe you didn't."

"I did."

"From Cromwell's description, I think you're the BenBugs guy involved with Birnam. Burch, is it? I'm not clear how you are involved in so much."

"Nevermind," said Patton and hung up. Seconds later, his phone rang again. He could see it was from the number he just called.

"Listen," said Patton, quickly moving to the hallway and the rear exit. "My lawyer and the FBI know exactly where I am."

"And so do I," said Josephs. "And you don't fully understand what's going on. I'm truly saddened about Samantha. If you stay there for a few more minutes, I'll meet you and explain. I own that restaurant, so my guys are on you. I promise you that you won't be hurt. You'll see things in a whole new light. Okay? Just be cool. I'll be right there."

When Patton hung up, he knew he was in deep shit. After he returned to the table, Tess walked back looking concerned. She sat and patted his hand. "I know you sometimes think I'm overly cautious, but we're in over our heads as it is."

"I agree."

She looked surprised. "So don't call Ernie Josephs."

"I already did," he said, "I'm sorry, but maybe it's a lucky thing."

"What? You talked with him?"

"Cromwell had called him immediately about Samantha, it turns out. I don't think Cromwell spoke about the mob stuff. However, this is Josephs' restaurant. He's coming to see us."

"Let's get out of here," she said, standing.

He didn't move. "His guys are to keep us here."

They cranked their heads around. A beefy waiter stood by the door smiling. A skinny guy in the kitchen met Patton's gaze and smiled.

"You know, you always think you're Mr. Nice Guy," said Tess, "but you're not always. You can be bullheaded. We shouldn't have even come here."

"I know."

"Did you just kill us, Patton?" said Tess.

CHAPTER 17

There had to be a way to escape. Two tables over, the professor sitting in front of a plate of steaming spaghetti told the young woman, "It's not that I'm anti-immigration, but we're spending far too much in social services on the illegals."

Patton turned to him, "You're feeding her head with conservative bullshit. If you took away the illegals in this valley, your wine industry would collapse. Is your head in a bubble or what?"

"I happen to teach economics, and your liberal make-believe world of help-the-poor at the expense of the rich is dooming the wetbacks to failure."

"The wetbacks! Take your Rush Limbaugh bubble and stick it up your ass."

"Patton!" said Tess.

"Fuck you, mister," said the professor, standing.

Patton grabbed the man's plate and dumped it over his head. Red ooze and noodles slid down the man's shocked face. Some of that slipped onto the young woman's blouse, and she screamed.

The man leaped over swinging, but he had too much sauce in his eyes, and he punched his date in the head, to more screams. Patton mashed the man's face in her mashed potatoes. The beefy guy near the front door ran over, and a closer, thinner waiter grabbed Patton around the waist. Patton elbowed him, and the waiter fell onto another table, sending dinners flying. More screams.

Everyone was up and running toward the front door, which stopped the beefy waiter and others. Patton grabbed Tess's hand and pulled her toward the hallway. "Come on," said Patton.

"I'm with you," she said.

They raced out the rear exit, only to see Ernie Josephs in a white suit and five young men in black jackets walk toward them.

"You're not leaving already, are you? Mr. Burch, is it?"

Patton froze. There were no guns visible, but each man had his hand in his jacket pocket. The beefy waiter and another came running toward them. Mr. Josephs waved them off.

"And this is Mrs. Burch?" said Josephs.

"Tess," said Tess. "And we just want to get out of here, okay?"

"Yes," said the man in white. "Join me in my car. We'll have a conversation, and then you'll be on your way."

Patton grabbed Tess, and started to run, but they only made a few steps before jacketed young men held them on either side.

Josephs ushered them into the back of his wide black Hummer H2, which matched a second one behind them. Tess slid in first, and Patton next to her. Josephs joined them.

"Drive," he said, and the car started off.

"Where are we going?" said Patton.

"A short drive," said Josephs. "You might want to put on your seatbelts." Josephs clicked his into place.

"What do you want from us?" said Tess, her voice mostly a whisper.

The car pulled out onto Highway 12 toward Sonoma. Soon, they turned at a light. Warm Springs Road said the sign.

"I think you two misunderstand me," said Josephs. "Whatever you think of me, I'm not that man. I'm a grape grower, nothing more. You were asking about a couple of murders."

"That's not our interest in the least," Patton blurted, heart pounding. Josephs' hand was in his coat. A gun?

"The murders came up in our research, but that's not why we're here," Tess added, her voice breaking.

"That's good to hear," said Josephs. "Not that I had anything to do with them, what with my alleged past and all." He took his hand out of his coat—free of any possible gun. "The fact that my accountant took advantage of me and then advantage of you is a real shame, too. It's not something I need publicized or even mentioned to the FBI—what with my alleged past and all. Have I come up in your chats with the FBI, Mrs. Burch?"

"How do you know I've spoken with them?"

"Ever since Birnam's been missing, I've spent considerable resources tracking just what he's done and where he might be. If the FBI hadn't been onto him, then you two would have been fine. He stole from me. So tell me, did the FBI mention me?"

"No. We didn't even know about you until today."

"That's the way I'd like to keep it. Let me tell you a little story of Anton Birnam and Samantha Malkey. Ms. Malkey was one of the most enthusiastic, talented, and gorgeous young women I've ever met. I predicted she had a good future. Birnam seemed to take a real interest in her, which I didn't know about. He had met her a few times when she came over on Naeper business, but I had no idea he'd seen her outside of business. Much later, I learned he was the one to take her away, convincing her that she had a better future with his help. I don't understand why she'd leave, frankly. He wasn't that charming, so God knows what story he invented. My wife and I, Samantha's parents, and Odell Naeper were surprised and confounded when she left—and Birnam never let on. I assumed her parents issued a missing person's report."

"They had not," said Patton. "They received a postcard from her saying she had left and would explain later. She told the same thing to her little sister in person."

"If Birnam hadn't been so greedy, taking so much of my money, I might not have ever known he was involved. My wife and I, all we want to do is grow grapes. I'm sure the FBI knows of me, but I'm not Birnam's only client or only rich client. If the FBI asks, I'd appreciate you saying you don't know anything about me."

"You could have told me that on the phone."

"No, I couldn't. These days, you don't know who the NSA or FBI is listening to."

"Hold it, hold it," said Patton. "Are you saying Birnam killed Samantha? I thought he really liked her and got her to Las Vegas."

"Best I can tell, she resisted his advances."

"So he killed her?"

"His universe was starting to unravel. He couldn't have her testify if it came to that. She must have known he was skimming funds—some of mine, but others', too."

"He seemed like such a nice guy," said Tess.

"He fooled me," said Josephs.

The car came to a stop in front of the restaurant. Josephs said, "So we all understand each other?"

"We're cool," said Patton. "Except where's Birnam now?"

"Between the FBI and me, I'm sure he'll be found."

— ❀ —

Back in the van, Patton and Tess rolled toward Boyes Hot Springs.

"I didn't expect Josephs to be so nice," Tess said.

"It was still a show of power. We don't want to cross him."

"You're right. Can't we just relax now, sit in a hot tub somewhere with a glass of wine?"

"I'm ready. Let's check into that spa place. It'll carry me through how many days I have to spend in prison until Birnam can be found and this whole thing cleared up."

"I'm sure Brian can keep you out."

"I'll call him later."

A few miles down the road, he turned in at Naeper.

"Now what're you doing?" Tess said.

"My computer, remember?"

"Why do you always try to cram so much in a day?"

"We're here. They're having a reception tonight, and I was told to pick up my computer at the front desk. I don't want to come tomorrow."

She sighed.

They passed under the arch for the Naeper Winery and veered left, up the hill, following the sign with an arrow that said "Waldorf-Crawford Wedding." In the darkening twilight, the sky glowed with puffs of vibrant orange clouds like Halloween marshmallows. The darkening valley showed street lights clicking on like various isolated stars.

Patton's van downshifted loudly into the lowest gear for the steepest portion of the driveway, and his engine revved. At the top, a line of cars swung around the fountain, and one long limo moved into the circle. Patton now saw they'd have to use the valet. There was no spot to park the van. "I'll stay in this line," he told Tess, "if you wouldn't mind dashing in and asking for my computer at the front desk."

"Okay." She left and soon returned, saying through the window, "No one's at the front desk. This place is gorgeous, though."

"Maybe I can find June," Patton said.

A valet in a white shirt and red vest approached his truck.

"We're here for a pick-up. We'll probably be no more than ten or fifteen minutes," he told the man. "Maybe you can keep it nearby?"

"We don't have no space up here," said the man.

"How about over there?" said Patton pointing.

"I'll try," said the man. It wasn't as if the van, though, was the look they were going for. Patton could guess it was a no. The man handed Patton a valet ticket.

CHAPTER 17

Patton told Tess he'd show her a little of the place.

"Goody," she said.

When they walked in behind another couple, Patton was surprised to see June LeCompte descending the stairs, dressed in an elegant organdy dress. "Welcome to Naeper," she told the couple in front of them. "Follow the signs out to the back."

When she saw Patton, she did a double-take. "Mr. Burch. This is a pleasant surprise," which sounded honest in her down-under accent. She shook his hand. "Do you know the betrothed?"

"Patton left his computer here," said Tess.

"The receptionist this morning said she'd have it here at the front desk," said Patton.

"Ah." She leaned in conspiratorially. "Is this your lovely wife?" said June, extending her hand to Tess.

"Yes. Tess, this is June LeCompte."

They shook hands.

"I'm chuffed," said June.

Tess frowned, and June laughed. "I keep forgetting it's not a word used here. 'Chuffed' means 'pleased.' What you Yanks might call 'stoked.'"

"She's Mr. Naeper's right-hand woman."

"That's what it says on my bloody business card, 'right-hand woman'. Let's get your computer."

June pointed more people in the direction of the terrace in the back then scooted behind the reception desk and looked for his computer under the desk. When it wasn't clearly around, she opened drawers.

"I'm sorry," said June. "She said it'd be here?"

"I thought so."

"Where did you leave it?"

"Up in the library."

"I can't leave here—do you mind going up? Remember the way?"

"Fourth door on the right. May I bring Tess to show her the library and maybe out back?"

June waved with a smile. "Heck, show away. Odell's gone anyway."

Another wave of people entered, so Patton took Tess by the hand to the staircase. When they walked into the library, it was dark, but the gas fireplace was on, which Patton thought odd. Wasn't that dangerous? He found the light switch by the door.

"Impressive room," said Tess. "Kind of makes our collection of books look like we're illiterate."

"I love where we live," said Patton.

"Me, too," said Tess, pulling him in, giving him a kiss.

He felt tingly and hoped she did, too. He leaned in and kissed her more passionately.

"Your computer?" said Tess.

"Right, right." He walked over to where he had sat with Odell and looked on the floor by the couch, but the computer wasn't there. He knelt down, looked under the couch. Not there. He stood and glanced around the room for his case, perplexed.

"I guess the receptionist got it, after all." His eyes came to Odell's desk. A computer just like his was opened and plugged in, standing next to a second laptop.

"Is that mine?" He strode right toward it. The case on the desk looked like his, too. As he swung around, he saw that his computer was in parts, actually. The bottom had been removed, and what appeared to be his hard drive was out and connected by wires to the other laptop. The other computer's screen was black, but the moment he touched the keyboard, it came to life.

"That's weird," said Patton.

"What?"

"My hard drive is out, and Odell was looking at it." He looked more carefully at what was onscreen. "My notes on my investigation."

"What's there for him to find out?"

"Notes on Samantha, her background, her parents. Not much. Why would he care? Birnam is our man."

A white sheet of paper next to the computer had handwritten notes, which Tess lifted up. "He searched me, too. He has my whole work history here and everything on BenBugs—the year it was incorporated, the names of everyone in the company."

It was only then that Patton noticed the book that had been beneath the sheet of paper. It was *How We Die* by Sherwin B. Nuland. A stem or something stuck out from the book, and he flipped the book open. A dried, flattened yellow rose lay there. He felt a surge as if he were sprinting. It wasn't Birham who had killed Samantha. This said it was Odell. He showed Tess.

"What?" she said.

"This is just like the flattened rose that was in Samantha's car. Now it makes sense. Birnam wasn't hiding Samantha from the mob or Josephs but actually protecting her from Odell."

"But why wouldn't she have asked Josephs? Why Birnam?"

"He was the one to take her out to dinner. Maybe Birnam then learned about Odell. Clearly Odell's a control freak."

Chapter 17

"And so Odell discovered where she was?"

"Yep. A year later."

"Now are you satisfied?" said Tess. "Is this enough to show the authorities?"

"I wonder if the copy of Lady Chatterley's Lover that was in Samantha's car is here? That would nail things. Odell surely killed the manager."

"Why?"

"Odell had given him the book for Samantha, and later, after she died, the manager caught Odell trying to get into her apartment. The manager was a witness." Patton pointed to the bookshelves. They started looking.

Tess went over to the one shelf with glass doors, then soon shouted "Aha!" She pulled out a book and handed it to Patton.

He examined the outside. "This is different," he said. "Not the new leather-bound one I saw." He opened Lady Chatterley's Lover, stopped at the title page, and read aloud, "To my stunning Odell, who is so focused on his wines and his power over people. You might love this book for its sex, but it's really about a woman who can decide her own fate. She is potent."

"Wow," said Tess. "Sounds like she was a little mad."

A tiny-flowered flattened plant slipped from the book. Patton reached to the floor for the mustard-looking thing, then examined it. "This may be ragweed. This book and plant is all we need."

"I never read the book," said Tess. "What's it about?"

"A young married woman in England becomes lonely when her upper-class husband becomes paralyzed and impotent. She takes on a lover, a games-keeper. They eventually marry—all very proper for having a lot of sex."

Odell's voice came from deep in the hallway. "June, why the hell do I need to go out there?"

Patton whispered loudly, "Odell. Hide. There's a closet over there." As Tess rushed toward the door, Patton lunged toward the light switches, hitting them off. He ran toward the closet, too, and just as he shoved in, flattening Tess behind him, Odell said, "You know I don't like these things." The sound of the light switches flipped on again.

"It helps with word-of-mouth," said June. "We need more bookings. You make everyone feel charmed and special."

"Hey, where's the computer?" said Odell.

"You mean Mr. Burch's computer?"

"Yes."

"I sent the Burches up here. He said it was supposed to be at the front desk for him. Didn't you know they were coming tonight?"

"I forgot to pack it up."

"You were using his computer?"

"I needed to see how much he knew," said Odell.

"Did he know anything?"

"Not really." He frantically looked around his desk. "I left my notes here about him—and a book."

"That's not good."

"We've got to find them."

"They're probably in the valet line if we hurry."

Their running footsteps soon echoed down the hall.

"I think there's some back stairs," whispered Patton in the closet, still holding the book. "Let's get out of here."

Tess followed him down the back, but they heard Odell's voice again approaching the back stairs from below. Odell said, "You stay out front by their van. I'll search upstairs and out back."

Patton reversed course, and they dashed down the hallway to the front stairs. They sped down when Tess said, "Promise me we'll have a nice boring life after this, okay?"

The front entryway was empty—June wasn't there—and they ran toward the front door. Once outside, Patton could see no more cars in line. The valets sat on the stairs, but Patton rushed past them because he could see his van parked right where he asked it to be, at the crest of the drive going down.

Patton twisted around, running back to the valets. "Are the keys in the van?" he gasped.

"Si, señor," said one man.

Patton yanked out his wallet, saw he had only a ten, and shoved it at the man. "Thanks," said Patton. "Hurry," he told Tess, and they sprinted.

They cranked open their doors at the same time. Patton avoided his seatbelt and simply started the van.

Tess slammed her door shut and tried to yank the seatbelt that wouldn't unspool fully. "Your fucking old car," she said.

"Hey," came Odell's shout, and Patton saw Odell running down the steps toward him with June not far behind.

Patton jammed the truck into drive and hit the accelerator. The rear view mirror showed Odell focused and running, almost to the van.

"Shit, it smells like gas," said Tess, opening her window. "Is your van broken again?"

"I don't know," he said, concentrating on zooming down the drive while opening his window, too. At the curve, he pressed the brakes—to no response. The pedal was limp, and hammering on it did nothing. He realized the brakes had been tampered with. He turned the steering wheel hard, but the van careened over as Tess was screaming "No!"

They slammed over the edge.

The van tumbled. Patton landed on the ceiling, then back in his seat, then back on the ceiling. He knew how perfectly they had just been set up. Odell had been expecting them and cut the brake line. That wasn't a random gas smell. That was a couple of gas cans clanging around with them, spraying gas over them as the van continued rolling. He heard Tess's screams diminishing as he realized she'd been thrown out the window. Next thing he knew, he was flying through the air, too. The van tumbled down the hill beyond him when a flash of light blew right toward him. The van was now a fireball, rolling until it came to a stop. They were supposed to be in there, frying.

He could hardly breathe now, realizing his landing on the ground had pounded the wind out of him. He fought for air. Is this the way he'd die? He concentrated, focusing on the moon above him. A bright star stood next to the moon. Too bright for a star. Venus. The star was Venus.

And then he breathed. Hard and long. He now realized why Odell wanted them to see all that stuff in the library—so they'd rush out of there. They had expected them. It'd been perfectly choreographed for them to slide over the hill. Odell had been a master. The valet probably took the van somewhere where the seatbelts were disabled, the brake lines cut, and the gas was added while he and Tess were in the library. It wouldn't surprise him if Odell had the place bugged, and he had heard every word. June was a part of it, too.

He could not hear Tess at all and had no idea what her condition was. Was she dead? Please, please, no.

He smelled gasoline. The liquid was on him, but he wasn't on fire. Barely able to move, Patton lifted up his head and could see the van, now just a black husk, still intensely burning. He heard the crunch of footsteps. "Tess?"

"No, Mr. Burch. Odell."

Patton turned his head. Odell's silhouette towered over him.

"You don't die easily, do you?" said Odell. "Your poor wife is probably burning down there, sorry to say. And in a second here, you'll join her."

Odell struck a match across its match book. A little flame quickly flared and died. Patton tried sitting up to run but the pain shot into his eyes as a white light. He must have broken some ribs.

"It's because of YOU that Samantha fled—control freak," Patton said.

"Control has its place," said Odell. "I'm in control of this next match, for instance, and you're covered in gasoline." He struck the match, which flared and, this time, stayed burning.

Still shuddering in pain, Patton felt around on the ground with one hand. He grabbed a rock, perfectly round. No, it was a golf ball. The lit match glowed in Odell's hand, and the single flame showed Odell grinning like some kid who enjoyed torturing pets.

Every nerve ending within Patton seemed to ignite a killing anger, focused into the power of his arm. Aiming for the oval of Odell's face, he threw the ball hard. There was a smack and Odell's scream, and Odell dropped the match. Patton turned with all his might to avoid the flame of the match. The pain from a broken bone returned again so vividly that Patton, too, screamed.

He opened his eyes, breathing hard, and saw he wasn't on fire. Odell, however, was staggering, still on his feet and holding his head. Then Tess's voice screamed, "Fuck you, mister!" and there was a punching sound. She must have kicked him hard from behind—her kickboxing finally coming into use—and Odell pitched forward right onto his face. He rolled like a rag doll down the steep hill. He came to rest against the burning hulk of the van, but there were no more sounds. No scream. Just his clothes starting to burn. Then his whole body.

"Are you okay, babe?" said Tess above him. Her dandelion kisses skated across his face. He tried to talk, but he was still having a hard time breathing—more difficult than before. Tess, the moon, Venus all became shrouded in black. He felt himself shake in uncontrollable shivering. He heard other footsteps coming and some sounds, but the sounds reverberated. He closed his eyes.

CHAPTER 18 (DAY 9)

A half-empty IV told Patton he was in the hospital. The room light was dim. A clock on the nightstand showed it was after three a.m. He cleared his throat and then heard movement.

"Feeling better?" said Tess, blinking away, now at his side. A chair that had been converted to a futon was to the side.

Tess turned on his bedside lamp. She wore a soft pink sweater. That was odd.

"You have a new sweater?" he said. "I never remember you ever wearing pink."

"My other sweater ripped on the hill," she said. "A little clothing store next to the car rental place had a few sweaters."

"You had time to rent a car?"

"Yes, and to talk to detectives, check us out of our hotel, and call Brian. Would you like some water?"

Patton nodded. "What have I been up to? All I remember is a doctor giving me a shot."

Tess held the cup and straw up to Patton's mouth, and Patton sipped. It was wonderfully wet. Wetness was an amazing thing, which he'd never considered before. He swished some water around his mouth before swallowing.

"Morphine," said Tess. "Apparently you're really sensitive to it, and you were just lyin' there with a smile on your face."

"That's because you didn't die."

She touched his face and smiled. "Only scratches," she said. "You, on the other hand, had a serious cut on your leg and lost a lot of blood. Two units. And you cracked your skull, two ribs, and broke your right foot."

He moved his right foot and could feel something tight around it, probably a cast. With a free hand, he felt around his chest. It felt very tender and painful, but there was nothing around him, no cast or bandages. Maybe there was nothing to do about a cracked rib.

"How long do I have to be here?"

"Maybe just one more day—make sure you're stabilized, they said."

"And that fucker Odell is dead?"

Tess nodded. "June told the police how Odell had said you'd killed Samantha, but she saw with her own eyes that he was going to burn you. She then realized he'd been so obsessed about Samantha, he did her in."

"She was in on it," he said.

"She knew nothing of his fixation or his going to Las Vegas. The police have confirmed he went to Vegas recently. June didn't think he was going to kill us—just confront us."

"Like I believe that."

"It's out of our hands. I spoke to Brian, who's coming in the morning. He'll take us to Las Vegas for an arraignment when you're checked out of here, and he'll put in a motion to dismiss. You didn't kill Samantha. You'll be free and clear."

He stared at his wife. "I'm so sorry, Tess. When our van tumbled and I realized having no seatbelts would probably kill us, I felt like choking God. Why is it life's so hard that good people can barely get through it in one piece? I can't believe we made it. Everything I put you through— please forgive me."

She nodded. "I'm sorry, too," she said. "Odd as it is, we have this together. How can we not be—like in that play we saw—'grappled together with hoops of steel'? I suppose when our days got so busy, it was easy to take you for granted. No more."

"You forgive me?"

She whispered, "Of course," and then kissed him.

— ❧ —

In the morning, his mother bustled in like a banker making sure the doors were opened on time.

"Mom!" said Patton from his bed.

"You're on the news. I flew up as fast as I could."

"You could've called. In fact, I know Tess was going to try."

"We talked."

Chapter 18

"So you didn't have to fly up."

"Of course I did—but you're not a parent, so you don't know these things."

"Now don't start in on that. I barely survived."

"You're so dramatic." She put her purse on the nightstand and started straightening other items on it.

"What're you going to do up here? I need to rest."

"We can play Parcheesi."

"You hate board games. I hate board games."

"We'll adapt. After all, you're a hero now."

"Ha! I'm just an average guy."

"Average guys don't figure out what the police couldn't." She smiled proudly.

"I was fighting for my life."

His mother tucked his blanket in more neatly at the bottom. "The good news is if all your signs remain stable today, the doctor said you can leave tomorrow. I grilled your doctor, you know. I want to make sure your pain is managed. Maybe you should stay here longer."

Patton purposely wrinkled his blanket. "Mom, I love you, but Tess is taking care of things. My pain's fine."

"Where's Tess?"

"Breakfast. As you probably heard, she was in the van, too, as it rolled, but she didn't break anything."

"Horrible, just horrible, what you two had to go through. Tess also called me during your troubles. Make sure you treat her well."

"I always do."

"Being married's hard for women. It's not as if we yearn to clean men's underwear or remind you to put your shoes away so we don't trip on them."

"You had to fly to tell me this?"

"With no disrespect to your father, may he rest in peace, but it's easier with him gone—and you, too. I put in my thirty-eight years, and now the house is the way I like it."

"I'm not sure what kind of marriage advice that is."

His mother shook her head while staring at the petite blonde nurse outside the door at a desk, writing. Eerily, the woman looked similar to the young woman Patton had seen his father with years ago.

"I'm saying nothing," said his mother.

Tess walked in at that moment, and said, "Westie! So good to see you."

"Thank you—and good to see you." They hugged, and the older Mrs. Burch turned to her son. "See, that's the way it's done, not 'You could've called.'"

Patton threw his hands in the air. "I give up."

The two women spent much of the morning with him, and then Tess took her mother-in-law to the nearby Hilton. Tess dissuaded her from going to Las Vegas with them and the lawyer. Mom was just going to spend one night before returning home.

"I have a surprise for you," Tess said when his dinner came.

"What?"

"Because we'll be in Las Vegas again and not working, I booked us a suite at The Venetian. You said you always wanted to try it."

"It's closer than the real Venice."

"We're there for three nights."

"It'll be our middle-aged honeymoon—with an IV." He lifted his IV line.

She whacked his hand. "That's coming out today."

"I like when you're so naughty," he said.

"I'm going to talk with your doctor and see how naughty I can be."

"I already asked. He said as long as I keep weight off my ribs, everything should be fine."

She pulled down her pants and underwear so fast, he didn't grasp what she was doing until she was in the narrow bed with him.

"Here? Now?" He looked around as if there might be someone there.

"You're not on a heart monitor or anything."

The door was closed. Dinner and rounds were over. She touched him in just the right spots.

Later, he could only think of how no one had ever explained that being married for fifteen years could be so good.

CHAPTER 19 (DAY 10)

B rian stood before Patton, unwrapping a protein bar. Tess was still asleep on the futon.

"You're a morning person, I take it," said Patton.

"Big day today. We have a 9:30 morning flight."

"Tess told me."

"Why aren't you guys up?"

"Maybe because it isn't even seven yet. How'd they let you in here?"

"I'm a lawyer," he said as if that explained anything.

Tess zipped into Patton's bathroom to spruce up. Patton passed on the breakfast so that they could all eat together. An hour later they were at the Sky Lounge restaurant at the Sonoma County Airport with his mother, who also managed to book an early flight.

Later, in Las Vegas, everything in the court went according to plan. When Patton, Tess, and Brian exited, a phalanx of photographers was on the courthouse steps. A forest of hands appeared with microphones held out.

"How did it feel to be accused of murder when you didn't do it?" said one newscaster in a suit, and for that, Patton had paused. "I knew Samantha Malkey only briefly, and she had a great heart. She will be missed by many people."

"Yes, but you were accused of killing her to cover up an affair, according to my source, and we hear you solved what really happened."

"Listen, I'm just a businessman selling beneficial bugs—BenBugs, the organic choice." Patton smiled to the camera.

"And you'd had sex with Ms. Malkey?" asked another reporter.

He shook his head. "My personal life is with my wife," said Patton. He held up his hand in Tess's.

They grabbed a single cab, dropping Brian off back at the airport before Patton and Tess went to The Venetian. On the airport curb, Patton said, "Brian, thank you for your patience. I know I must have driven you crazy, but I appreciate you sticking with me."

"I couldn't disappoint your mom. Don't forget to call her with the news."

"I won't. I'll have to call our employees, too."

"You're formidable, Patton. You're right, you drove me crazy, but it's been an honor to work with you." They shook hands. "Bill will be in the mail."

Now in the mild temperature of the Venetian, Patton lay in their king-size bed with a fluffy comforter. Tess had wanted to do a lot: get her hair and nails done, buy a new dress, and stop at another drugstore. She nonetheless seemed distracted. She'd meet him in a few hours at a restaurant in St. Mark's Square.

He clomped in his walking cast to the room's windows that overlooked the pools ten stories down. One pool was extremely shallow and filled mostly with women lying on lounge chairs immersed in the water. The other pool was only chest deep and had people, mainly couples, standing and chatting. Vegas appealed to couples. He was starting to believe he was a "couple" again.

That morning at the hospital, however, Tess had seemed preoccupied, distant even. It was after she'd gone down to the pharmacy to pick up his medicine. She'd taken a while and said there'd been a line. He'd assumed she was anxious about the court meeting, but she'd seemed similarly tentative afterward and hardly spoke in the cab. Something was off despite her professing "hoops of steel" the day before.

Maybe she was feeling something similar as first falling in love: you were sure of the love but lost sleep that so much happiness would be cut. The sword of Damocles swayed just above you. After all, the person you loved might say something that would shred everything, such as, "I thought I was ready for a relationship, but I'm not," or "Monogamy isn't for me," or "I like you, but I'm just not a commitment-type of person." Maybe Tess thought he harbored doubts. She shouldn't be so anxious.

Perhaps it was the aftereffects of their traumatic event. Maybe she was having post-traumatic stress. He wasn't, but that didn't mean she wasn't. Something was bothering her.

It was still a few hours before meeting her, but the Venetian Hotel was so large, with three Broadway-size legitimate theatres, a handful of night-clubs, clothing stores, and eighteen elegant restaurants, that he wanted to find San Marcos Square in advance. The in-room guide said it was by the Grand Canal Shoppes, which were on the second floor.

After he exited the elevator on the second floor, he came to the Grand Canal, real water in a Venice-like waterway a story over the casino. A handsome gondolier poled a canal boat with two couples in it past a café and a few shops. Patton stared. Here, the air was a chilled seventy, while outside, the real sun relentlessly pounded the desert, trying to crush every living thing. Here, high overhead, a blue sky had been painted on the concave ceiling with a bird in the distance, forever stuck in the azure.

This was Venice by way of Hollywood, yet there were no film cameras or a sound stage, and he wasn't part of an audience in the dark. The whole place was a trick of the eye, trompe l'oeil, crafted illusion.

And he wondered what was so bad about that? We all needed a little illusion to float us to a better place. This life was hard enough for anyone—why begrudge a fantasy?

As he moved past the shops and by many couples holding hands, he began to see things differently. Samantha had been killed not by anything he'd done but because someone, Odell, had wanted to own her, to have all the control. Patton realized he couldn't control Tess's feelings, let alone his own.

As his cast punctuated his steps on the tile floor, people smiled at him as if he was feeling what they were feeling, a shared hope. Maybe that's what all we needed, he thought—optimism despite aging and disease. Today, after all, he was in The Venetian, happy, healing, and about to celebrate.

He came to a big area, a large square—a version of St. Mark's Square, but the square's tiles gleamed, highly polished, unlike the one in Italy. More tricks for the eye. The sunlight came from hidden lamps and offered a friendly late afternoon presence. Over to the right, a white-faced clown, ten-feet tall on stilts, walked nodding to those in a café. People clapped. On the other side on a small stage, a young man played flute and a woman next to him sang in Italian. People watched, enthralled. At another outdoor café, Postrio, the one where he was to meet Tess, a young couple kissed. In the bustle of real people, Patton felt a tap on his shoulder. He swung around. Tess looked apprehensive still. Lord, no. Say it ain't so.

"What are you doing here?" they both said at the same time.

"Checking out where we're meeting," said Tess.

"Me, too."

"Good minds think alike."

"I hope so."

Yet doubt hung on her face. If worry were Crisco, she could have fried a thousand fries. "Patton, there's something I have to tell you."

Here it was. He hadn't been imagining it. His instincts had been right. "What?" he said, caressing one of her shoulders, trying to reassure her that he could be depended upon.

"You may not be happy to hear this, so I've been worrying. I also had to be sure."

"We're a great couple," said Patton. "If I learned anything, I can't rule you. I've never been the king-type anyway. You are your own person. I just want to be with you."

She frowned. "Just me?"

"Of course."

She frowned again.

"I know I have to regain your trust, but perhaps in time—"

"You're already there," she said. "I trust you. I thought you got that yesterday. You misunderstand me."

"I'll get better at understanding," he said.

"Wherever you're head's at, get out of it," she said. She pulled a little thermometer from her purse, and it had a plus sign on it. A second one had a dark dot. Because he'd been expecting something else, this threw him.

"Do you hate me?" she said.

"I'm sorry. Is this—what?—a pregnancy thing?"

She nodded and grimaced as if she hated to hear what he was going to say.

"I thought you were on the pill."

"I stopped. I thought I was going through menopause, so I didn't think I could get pregnant. Besides, we didn't make love that often."

"After the party was great. So was the other night."

"I missed my period a week ago. Today I thought I'd check."

"Are these things that accurate?"

"Not necessarily this early. Still, I missed my period."

In that moment, he understood what he wanted—and what he hoped she wanted. "Hey! We can be parents?"

She nodded. He nodded. He was both excited and afraid, the feeling so clear, a vision that Carlos Casteñada might have. He saw his future. Through illusion comes truth.

The clown on stilts, a mime, approached them, and Tess raised her arms in the air enthusiastically. Patton joined raising his hands and danced a victory dance. The clown raised his arms exaggeratedly, then put his hand to his ear, inviting them to speak. Instead, Tess put her hands to her tummy, miming, too, and then pointed to Patton and herself. Patton pretended to hold a baby in his arms, swinging it.

The clown whistled to get everyone's attention nearby, and the clown re-mimed what Tess and Patton had done. The applause made Patton smile.

Tess kissed him hard. "Do you mean it?" she asked back.

"I do."

And so they were joined in a whole new way, there in St. Mark's Square.

Acknowledgments

Thank you to my great editor, Lynn Hightower, as well as my many initial readers including Barry Martin at Book 'Em bookstore, Carol Fuchs, Jim McCarthy at the Dystel-Goderich Agency, David Pibel, Steve Hazzard, and Paula White. Thank you also to Deborah Daly, whose work and enthusiasm goes beyond design and who, in this book, came up with a better title than the one I had—one that market research also agreed with. The title *A Death in Vegas* gave her a better bedrock to lay her design on and allowed me, in my final rewrite, to center on it, too.

And finally, thank you to my wife, Ann Pibel, whose support, easy-going nature, and smarts mean a lot.

About the Author

Christopher Meeks has four novels and two collections of short fiction published. His most recent novel is the acclaimed thriller, *Blood Drama*. His novel *The Brightest Moon of the Century* made the list of three book critics' Ten Best Books of 2009. *Love at Absolute Zero* also made three Best Books of 2011 lists, as well as earning a *ForeWord Reviews* Book of the Year Finalist award.

He has had stories published in several literary journals, and the stories have been included in the collections *Months and Seasons* and *The Middle-Aged Man and the Sea*. Mr. Meeks has had three full-length plays mounted in Los Angeles, and one, *Who Lives?*, was nominated for five Ovation Awards, Los Angeles' top theatre prize.

Mr. Meeks teaches English and fiction writing at Santa Monica College, and Children's Literature at the Art Center College of Design. To read more of his books visit his website at: www.chrismeeks.com.

Praise for Christopher Meeks's previous novels:
Love At Absolute Zero

ForeWord Reviews' BOOK OF THE YEAR FINALIST

TOP-TEN BEST FICTION 2011 at *Book Chase*.
"It is impossible not to like Gunnar Gunderson. As he progresses from one disaster or near miss to the next, one views him with a mixture of compassion and laughter.

> —**Sam Sattler**, *Book Chase* blog

Winner 2011 *Red Adept Reviews* Indie Award—Romance: "The author hit a home run. It's a very good story, very well told."

> —**Jim Chambers**, *Red Adept Reviews*

Winner 2011 Noble Award (not Nobel): "The tension between science and emotion has never been more keenly felt."

> —**Carolyn Howard-Johnson**

"Thermodynamics are nothing; it's that love thing that is so frustrat- ingly hard to figure out. *Love at Absolute Zero* is an excellent read that is very much worth considering, highly recommended!"

> —*Midwest Book Review*

"It is a given, now, that Christopher Meeks is a master craftsman as a writer. The novel is a gift—and one of the many that continue to emerge from the pen and mind of so genuinely fine a writer."

> —**Grady Harp**, Amazon Top-Ten Reviewer

"Three cheers for Christopher Meeks and his wildly entertaining pica- reque novel about the gentle, bumbling hero physicist Gunnar Gundar- son's quest for love and marriage."

> —**Linda Hitchock**, BookTrib

"As engaging as it is amusing, *Love at Absolute Zero* is, ultimately, a heartfelt study of the tension between the head and heart, science and emotion, calculation and chance."

> —**Marc Schuster**, *Small Press Reviews*

"A deeply resonant read that manages to be funny without sacrificing its gravity. Highly recommended!"

> —**Heather Figearo**, *Raging Bibliomania* blog

Months and Seasons and Other Stories:

"The stories in *Months and Seasons* are like potato chips: you can't read just one."

—Marc Schuster, *Small Press Reviews*

"With this collection, Christopher Meeks proves there is an audience for short stories. His characters are well defined with problems that they can't resolve. Meeks's stories reminded me of those of John Cheever."

—Gary Roen, *The Midwest Book Review*

"*Months and Seasons*, not only will not disappoint, but also it will provide further proof that we have a superior writer of the genre in our presence."

—Grady Harp, Top Ten Reviewer, Amazon.com

"Full of complete randomness and quirkiness, ingredients I cherish, the stories in this twelve-story collection chronicle the eccentricities of an array of diverse characters, who are dealing with life thrown at them in the only way actually possible: by dealing with their problems, not escaping them."

—Rachel Durfor, *Rebecca's Reads*

"I am pleased to report that if *Months and Seasons*, the new collection from Christopher Meeks, was a music album, many of its twelve pieces would be destined for the charts – no filler here."

—Sam Sattler, *Book Chase* blog

"*Months and Seasons* is a wonderful collection of short stories that reminded me why it is that I enjoy short fiction so much. "

—Rebecca Schinsky, *The Book Lady*

"*Months and Seasons*, the second short story collection from Christopher Meeks, is a exceptionally entertaining and thought-provoking offering from a gifted writer."

—Heather Figearo, *Raging Bibliomania* blog

The Brightest Moon of the Century

"Christopher Meeks chronicles one man's path to middle-age and, in doing so, illustrates how choices and circumstances—even those that seem arbitrary and the time—have a way of irrevocably cementing a person's future."

—**Cherie Parker**, *Minneapolis Star Tribune*

"This is a moving novel."

—**Rachel Durfor**, *Rebecca's Reads*

"Charming and endlessly entertaining."

—*Midwest Book Review*

"Throughout it all, Meeks uses Edward's worries and internal dialogue as a focus to show the possibilities found in small moments: in sun-rises, in friendships, in apparent disaster. Unpretentious and deeply human, the normalcy and everyman nature of the novel give it power."

—**Jennie Blake**, *BookGeeks*

"This is what I love about Meeks: his ability to gauge humanity, his understanding and acceptance of the strangeness of intricacies of life and personality, and his wonderful sense of compassion for his charac- ters."

—**Heather Figearo**, *Raging Bibliomania*

"I have to say I've gone from being an admirer of his work to a full-blown fan bordering on groupie."

—**Marc Schuster**, *Small Press Reviews*

"His stance in the echelon of new important American writers seems solidly secure."

—**Grady Harp**, Top Ten Amazon Reviewer

"Meeks has the talent to carry his quirky characters and their 'find their extraordinary in the everyday' plots into a full-length novel."

—**Dawn Rennert**, *She's Too Fond of Books*

"[Meeks] gives us characters who are very human and who face many obstacles in life, and then he infuses their stories with hope."

—**Wendy Robards**, *Caribousmom*